OUT OF THE ASHES

A Shelby Belgarden Mystery

OUT OF THE ASHES

Valerie Sherrard

A BOARDWALK BOOK
A MEMBER OF THE DUNDURN GROUP
TORONTO · OXFORD

Editor: Barry Jowett
Copy Editor: Andrea Pruss
Design: Jennifer Scott
Printer: Webcom

Canadian Cataloguing in Publication Data

Sherrard, Valerie
      Out of the ashes

ISBN 1-55002-382-9

I. Title.

PS8587.H3867O98 2002   C813'.6   C2002-901071-3   PZ7.S5458Ou 2002

       3   4   5   06   05   04   03

THE CANADA COUNCIL | LE CONSEIL DES ARTS
FOR THE ARTS | DU CANADA
SINCE 1957 | DEPUIS 1957

ONTARIO ARTS COUNCIL
CONSEIL DES ARTS DE L'ONTARIO

We acknowledge the support of the **Canada Council for the Arts** and the **Ontario Arts Council** for our publishing program. We also acknowledge the financial support of the **Government of Canada** through the **Book Publishing Industry Development Program**, **The Association for the Export of Canadian Books**, and the **Government of Ontario** through the **Ontario Book Publishers Tax Credit** program.

Care has been taken to trace the ownership of copyright material used in this book. The author and the publisher welcome any information enabling them to rectify any references or credit in subsequent editions.

J. Kirk Howard, President

Printed and bound in Canada.⊕
Printed on recycled paper.

www.dundurn.com

Dundurn Press	Dundurn Press	Dundurn Press
8 Market Street	73 Lime Walk	2250 Military Road
Suite 200	Headington, Oxford,	Tonawanda NY
Toronto, Ontario, Canada	England	U.S.A. 14150
M5E 1M6	OX3 7AD	

This book is dedicated with love, admiration, and pride to my daughter, Pamela Sarah.

CHAPTER ONE

"For the last time, I'm not interested!" I guess I sounded pretty rude, but I just couldn't help it. It must have been, as my mom would say, the umpteenth dozen time I'd told Betts that I just plain didn't care how often Greg told his friends he thought I was special.

After all, Greg wasn't my type. He would never be my type. This is not to say I knew for sure what my type was at that point in my life, but I was one hundred percent certain he wasn't it.

We were walking home from class, and Betts was making yet another attempt to help me see that Greg was the Man of My Dreams. This is one of her favourite expressions this year, and I can tell you it was starting to wear on my nerves. Betts herself proclaimed that she'd found the Man of Her Dreams at least four times a week, and each time it was a new fellow. If that wasn't bad enough, she'd decided she was best qualified to pick out the Man of My Dreams for me. Even that might not have been so bad if she'd picked someone other than Greg. He'd been nothing but a source of humiliation to me almost from the first time I'd met him.

I guess I'm making Betts sound pretty boy crazy. Well, she does tend to be that way. But Betts has been my best friend since the fourth grade, and she's got oodles of other good qualities. I do my best to overlook her crazy notions because I think she invents all this romance in order to spice things up here in Little River.

I have to admit, this isn't the most exciting place to live. It's the kind of town where nothing much ever seems to happen, and sometimes you get the impression that the whole place is half asleep. The inhabitants, all five thousand of them, go about their business in a sort of mechanical way, as if they're characters in a movie where the same scenes are played over and over.

Not that it isn't a nice place. It is. My mom says it's the kind of town that picture postcards are made of, with a lot of big old homes that were built around the turn of the century. The streets are wide and clean, except for in the autumn, when the leaves float down from all the trees. We have so many trees that in the fall the whole place takes on the mottled colours of a yellow-orange cat. Then the residents come out with garbage bags that look like pumpkins, and before you know it there are grinning orange faces everywhere.

Our only sources of entertainment are the bowling alley and a movie theatre where, unlike big theatres, there's only one show playing at a time. With so little to do, the kids in town mostly hang out at each other's places or spend time at the soda shop.

There's a river running along the outskirts of the north side of town, and it's just about as lazy as the town itself. Most of the time there's hardly a ripple on the water, which is probably why canoes are the most popular of the boats that you see drifting along during the summer. Betts likes to talk about how romantic canoes are too!

Anyway, this whole story really started about four months ago. It seems only fair to go back to the beginning.

The funny thing about the beginning of a story is that it can be pretty hard to find. It might have been the first day of school in September, when I vaguely noticed a new guy in the cafeteria at school. In a small town like Little River, that's news. But in all honesty, I hadn't paid much attention to Greg Taylor at the time.

I can tell you though, if I'd known what kind of mess lay ahead, I would have taken greater notice.

He was a grade ahead of me, so he wasn't in any of my classes, which turned out to be a blessing. The way events shaped themselves over the school year, I'd have hated having to sit next to him in a classroom. It was hard enough avoiding him in the hallway when things started getting weird.

I'd been really excited about school this year. It was my first year in the high school, which was a big deal in itself. Also, I'd gotten my braces off during the summer and had finally, as Mom said, blossomed a little. I'd been waiting for both of those events for years!

I'm no Marilyn Monroe, don't get me wrong. But at least there are a few curves on the landscape now, which took their good old time in arriving.

I figured that with these new developments, this would be the best year I'd had so far. I'd been sweet on Nick Jarvis for a couple of years and thought maybe he'd finally notice that I existed. Actually, he already knew, but not in a good way, thanks to Betts. I'd made the mistake of confiding in her, and the next thing I knew, every time he passed me in the halls his friends would nudge him with their elbows, and he'd roll his eyes and pull a few faces.

I'd burn with shame when that happened, but I couldn't really blame him. After all, Nick is a jock, and a darned good looking one at that. He can pretty much take his pick of the girls, and that's what he's done. It always encouraged me to see that he never stuck with any one girl in particular but dated loads of them. In my heart I knew that when the Breast Fairy, as Betts puts it, finally visited me, he was going to realize that he'd been waiting for me all along.

Then the romance of the century would be ignited, and the rest would be history, a story that ended with "Happily Ever After." At least, that's what kept me going and helped me get past all the jeers from Nick and his friends in the junior high years.

So there we all were at the start of tenth grade, and there I was, Shelby Belgarden, who had never had one single date, ever. I was ready. Romance was sure to come calling, and I was going to be right there to let it in.

My mom gave me lots and lots of the parent talk thing, those long lectures on nice girls and not chasing boys and so on. Some of what she said made pretty good sense, and the rest was, I figured, part of her job as a mother. Sometimes Dad joined in the conversations, but in an embarrassed way that made it hard not to giggle right in front of him.

One of the things that really sunk in from all those "mother-daughter talks" was that if you let a boy know you like him, it might just scare him away. I'd seen the proof of that in action when Betts got the word out that I was into Nick. It had taken some doing to persuade her that I'd lost interest in him, but I'd managed it. Now, I figured that if I just played it cool, he'd come around.

I clearly remember Betts and me sitting in the cafeteria that first day of school. She noticed Greg right away. Betts notices everything!

"Who's that?" she whispered, pointing across the room at him.

I grabbed her hand and hauled it back down onto the table. Looking in the direction she'd indicated, I saw that she was pointing to the new guy. There was nothing particularly remarkable about him. He had dark hair and appeared to be of average height.

"Beats me," I said, noticing that Nick had just walked into the cafeteria and was sitting down beside Jane Goodfellow. She was tossing her head back and laughing in what I couldn't help but see was a pretty phony way. Jane is nothing if not phony, so this came as no surprise.

"He must be the son of that weird guy who moved into the old Carter house," Betts was speculating. "The only other new people in town are the couple who bought the drugstore from Jake's dad, and they're too young to have a kid in high school."

"Who?" I asked, distracted by the sight of Nick leaning over close to Jane. His smile was all over her, and it made my stomach hurt.

"The guy. The new guy." Betts' voice was exasperated. "Where's your brain gone off to anyway? What else were we talking about?"

"Oh, yeah, I guess so." I vaguely resurrected what she'd just said. "What makes you say his dad is weird?"

"Everyone knows about that," she half groaned. "How is it that you never hear anything that's happening in town?"

"I dunno. I guess I have better things to do than listening to gossip."

"Oh, for sure." Betts was laughing now. "Your life is just so full of exciting things and all. I can see why big news to everyone else is of no importance to you."

"Mmmmmm." Nick was touching Jane now! His hand was resting on her shoulder. I silently put the curse of a thousand zits on her, something that usually cheered me but didn't seem to help today. "So, tell me what's so weird about this guy's dad then, since you're just dying to force this information on me."

"He goes around town quoting poetry!" Betts' eyes were triumphant as she passed on this bit of news. I guess she figured it was pretty darned interesting.

"So?" I knew I was taking out my misery over Nick and Jane on her, since my tone of voice was getting nasty, but I couldn't help it.

"So, you don't think that's kind of odd?" Betts was picking up her lunch tray, and her face had a hurt look on it. I felt sorry right away and offered her one of my mom's chocolate chip cookies to make amends.

"I guess that is weird," I said. She brightened up and told me a few stories about this stranger moving to town and breaking into poems on a number of shopping trips.

"Mrs. Wells said she was half afraid of him. She said it was downright scary how he came in for a grocery order and started going on like a crazy person, reciting some poem about birch trees when she complained that there were kids climbing the trees in the town square."

"Robert Frost," I named the author automatically.

"*What* are you talking about? Who is this Robert guy?"

"Never mind." We'd taken one of his poems the year before, and I liked it so much that I read some others he'd written, including "Birches." But I knew Betts thought poetry was stupid and wouldn't remember it.

"Where does he work?" I asked, bringing her back to what we'd been talking about. I couldn't help wondering how she'd managed to hear all these things about someone I hadn't even known existed. Betts and her family had been away visiting relatives for the whole month of August and had just arrived back in town a few days before the start of school.

"That's another thing. He doesn't work. He only leaves the house when he goes to a store or to the post office. No one knows where he gets his money. Maybe he's some sort of criminal and he's hiding out in Little

River!" Betts seemed excited at that idea, as if it would be a great thing, but I found it a bit much.

"Well, in that case, we'd better steer clear of the criminal's offspring," I whispered ominously, nodding toward the new kid.

I had no idea how much I'd come to mean those words!

CHAPTER TWO

Betts is like a dog with a bone sometimes. She just grabs onto an idea or bit of information and never lets go until she figures she's gotten as much as possible out of it.

I knew that she wouldn't rest until she had the complete lowdown on the new boy in town, and I was right. She'd make a great investigative reporter if she ever had the opportunity.

It was the very next day that she had more to tell me. Goodness only knows where she gets her information, but she sure does get it.

"Shelby. Shelby!" I heard my name called from somewhere in the crowded hallway of the school. Her face appeared a few seconds later, and I could see right away that she was fairly bursting with news.

"Hey, Betts. What's up?" I asked, knowing full well she didn't need any prompting.

"I was right!" Her eyes were lit up, just like my Aunt Milly's get when she has that important air of someone with something to tell. "His father is the crazy person who bought the Carter house. And he has no mother. I don't know what happened to her."

"Maybe they killed off the mother and are living on the insurance money," I suggested. I knew it was a rotten thing to say, especially to Betts, who can take an idea like that and turn it into absolute fact in about two minutes.

She seemed to be considering this for a second, but other news pushed the thought aside. "His name is Greg Taylor, and he just got a job at Broderick's gas station. He works there after school on Tuesday and all day Saturday."

"How do you find these things out?" I wondered out loud.

"Easy, my mom was talking to Old Man Broderick's wife at the hairdresser's yesterday, and she told her all about Greg. Mrs. Broderick said that Greg came in looking for a job last week, and her husband hired him."

"I thought you said they were rich or something, that his father didn't have to work."

"All I said was that he didn't work. I didn't say they were rich. I wish you'd get things straight every once in a while," Betts smirked at my apparent inability to grasp things.

Thank goodness the bell rang then and spared me from a more detailed explanation of my shortcomings in the gossip department.

It was later in the week that I actually had my first encounter with Greg. At that time I still just thought of him as just the new kid and had no idea of the problems that lay ahead, so there was no reason not to be nice to him.

Thursday afternoon Betts and I stopped at The Scream Machine for orange floats. The Scream Machine was someone's idea of a catchy name for a soda shop. I think it came from the old saying "I scream, you scream, we all scream for ice cream." The teens in Little River hang out there evenings and weekends, so we were lucky to get a booth all to ourselves.

I was stirring the ice cream into my float and half listening to Betts, who was going on about Victor Mallory. Victor was the Man of Her Dreams at that moment, though his turn in this lofty position would be short-lived.

Anyway, right in the middle of sighs and comments about how absolutely perfect he was, she got this startled look on her face, leaned forward, and whispered, "He's here!"

I thought she meant Victor, since she was talking about him, but when I glanced up I saw it was the new kid. Not wanting to seem nosy, I pretended to be engrossed in the menu as he headed past our table on his way to the counter. And then Betts opened her mouth!

"Hey there." She was smiling up at him.

"Uh, hi." He offered a shy smile in return and then stood there as if he wasn't sure what to do next.

"Wanna join us?" Betts slid over as she spoke, clearing enough room in our booth for him to sit down.

"Sure." He sat down and immediately held his hand out toward Betts. "I'm Greg Taylor."

"Betts Thompson." She shook it quickly, then pulled her hand free and waved in my direction. "This is my very best friend Shelby Belgarden."

"Hi, Shelby." He offered me his hand then, and I shook it, but it felt strange. It seemed like something only adults did, and I was half worried someone would see me.

"So you're new in town," Betts commented. I felt almost sorry for Greg at that moment. I knew she was going to try to weasel information from him, which she would then pass on to anyone who would listen.

"Yeah. My dad and I came here last month. It's a nice place."

"Where did you live before?" Betts asked.

"Different places," he replied. "Say, what do you recommend here? Is the food good?"

I wondered why he'd answered so evasively and if changing the subject right afterward had been deliberate. I knew that Betts was thinking the same thing and that it would only make her more determined to find out anything she could about him.

I suddenly wanted to rescue him from her prying and started talking about just about everything they had on the menu. He looked at me oddly, and I couldn't blame him, as I raved about how nice and crisp their fries were, how juicy their burgers were, how I didn't favour their chowders but their homemade soups were usually not bad, and on and on.

Betts gave me a positively murderous look as I rambled endlessly. Greg just sat and stared and made an attempt to appear interested in each and every food item I talked about.

The waitress came before I was finished, and he ordered a burger and fries. As she turned from the table he added, "Make that to go, please."

"Are you leaving?" Betts asked, with the look of someone who had been cheated.

"Uh, yeah, I have to get back to the house. I promised my dad I'd give him a hand with some bookcases tonight."

"Bookcases?" Betts asked as though it was a new word to her.

"Well, we have a lot of books to unpack, and he needs some of them right away, so I want to help him get them ready. We've been putting it off while we got settled in, but it can't wait any longer."

Betts looked puzzled, as though she knew there was something she ought to ask about this urgent need for books but couldn't quite figure out what the question should be.

"Well, it's nice that you're helping your father," I said. "My mom has a lot of books too. My dad keeps saying that if she keeps buying more, we're going to have to build a few extra rooms just to hold them all."

"Do you read much yourself?" Greg asked me.

"That's all she does," Betts said before I could answer. She was rolling her eyes. "I keep telling her there are other things in life, but she's always got her nose stuck in some silly book."

"You think books are silly?" Greg asked her.

"It's bad enough that your teachers make you read a bunch of stupid stories for school," Betts replied. "I don't know why anyone would waste their time reading stuff they didn't have to."

"There's nothing wrong with reading." I felt my face getting hot. "It makes me feel as though I'm sort of escaping for a while."

That sounded pretty dumb, even to me, and I knew Betts was going to poke more fun at me for saying it. But before she got the chance, Greg spoke up and said, "I know exactly what you mean, Shelby. I read a lot too. In fact, I'd rather read than watch television."

"Oh, great, I'm here with a couple of freaks of nature," Betts moaned. She looked around and with a teasing laugh, added, "Are there any normal people in here that I can go sit with?"

Greg ignored this and said to me, "It looks like we have something in common. Maybe we can lend each other some of our favourite books."

I should have refused right then and there, but it seemed like a harmless suggestion, so I told him that would be nice. Just then the waitress came with his order, and he paid and left. As he went out the door he waved to me and called out, "Don't forget!"

In spite of the reminder, I soon forgot about his suggestion. How was I to know that something as innocent as swapping books was going to become a source of school gossip?

Chapter Three

When I got home that night there was a surprise waiting for me. It was a shelf unit Dad had made to hold all my stuffed animals, which had been piled all over the place. There were three sections: one in the middle, with two lower shelves on each side. It was really cool, painted blue with pale purple flecks to match my walls. Once we put it up I spent hours rearranging and organizing my room.

With all the activity, I never gave another thought to Greg or sharing books until school on Monday. I was at my locker getting my things ready for first class when I heard his voice.

"Shelby! I have some books for you."

I turned to see him standing beside me with four books in his arms. In fact, everyone around turned and looked. There was a sudden silence in the locker area.

"These four are great." He was smiling and didn't seem to notice that there was a very interested audience in the background. "I figured you've probably read most of the classics, so I picked more modern books."

"Uh, thanks." I mumbled, taking them from him. I noticed that the one on top was Frank McCourt's *Angela's Ashes*, which I'd read not long ago. I'd loved it and found myself irrationally annoyed at the thought that his taste was apparently similar to mine. Then I realized he was standing there waiting.

"I haven't had a chance yet to pick out anything for you," I tried to keep my voice low so that the other students couldn't hear. "It was a busy weekend."

"That's okay, no rush," he said pleasantly. "I just hope you enjoy these as much as I did. I couldn't put them down."

Giggles started then, along with oohs and aahs. He became aware of the stares we were getting. Instead of getting embarrassed, like any normal human being, he got an intense look on his face and said, "Perhaps they have never been where we have been. They laugh because they don't know our secret places. Don't let them bother you, Shelby. To thine own self be true."

Our secret places! To thine own self be true! I could have crawled into my locker and stayed there for the rest of the school year! The teasing started then and went on all day. It spread through the school faster than

24

you can imagine. Everywhere I turned I heard those two phrases repeated. I did my best to ignore the whispers and hoped it would just go away.

Betts cornered me at lunch. "What is all this talk about you and Greg and secret places? Are you holding out on me? Where did you two go this weekend? And why didn't you tell me about it?"

"Honest, Betts, I swear I didn't see him again until today. I never even gave him another thought. He brought me some books this morning and made some remarks that everyone took the wrong way." I didn't know how I could explain to her that the secret places he mentioned were in the books. I knew what he meant, but there was no way I could make her understand.

"Okay, if you don't want to tell me, that's fine." She looked hurt and kind of angry.

"Betts, wait!" I implored, but she was walking away and didn't even turn around.

I started to eat my lunch alone amid snickers and comments that were loud enough for me to hear. The worst part of it was that Nick looked at me and laughed a couple of times. He was leaning over and whispering to his friends, and I knew they were all talking about me and Greg. It wasn't fair. And there was no way for me to clear myself.

All I could do was hope the talk would die off when people saw that I wasn't hanging around with Greg. I

kept my head down, ignoring the talk around me, trying to pretend that my sandwich was the most fascinat-
ing thing in the world. And then it got worse.

"Hey, there. Want some company?"

I looked up to see Greg standing with his lunch in
his hand. Before I could open my mouth to tell him I'd
rather be alone at the moment, he plopped down in the
seat across from me and spread his food on the table.

I was embarrassed to tell him what everyone was
saying about us. Mainly, I was afraid that he'd say or do
something that would give everyone more ammunition
to add to the gossip. I concentrated on eating my lunch
and not looking at him.

"I wanted to thank you for last week," he said all of
a sudden.

"What do you mean?" I'd meant to pretty much
ignore him, but curiosity got the better of me.

"You know, at the soda shop, when your friend
was trying to get the goods on me and you talked and
talked so she didn't have a chance to ask a whole lot
of questions."

I hadn't realized he'd known what Betts was up to
or that I'd been talking so much to save him from her
prying. But I wasn't about to sell my best friend out by
admitting that to him. Even though she was being pretty unfair to me at the moment, I wasn't going to turn
on her! Especially not for him.

"I don't know what you mean," I said shortly.

He looked at me carefully and then just said, "Okay, my mistake."

I'd like to say that we ate in silence and then he went away and never bothered me again. That didn't happen.

"If a tree falls in the woods, and there's no living thing around to hear it, does it make a sound?" He popped this out of the clear blue as though it was a perfectly normal question.

"What?" I asked, startled.

"That's a question my dad used to ask his classes at university. He gives me things like that to think about, but he won't tell me what he thinks the answer is. I just thought you might help me figure it out."

"It's a pretty strange question," I said and then wondered out loud, "Your dad taught at a university?"

"Until last year," he told me.

I wanted to ask him why his father had left a good job like that and come to Little River. There had to be a pretty big reason for anyone to make that kind of change in their life. But I didn't want to seem like Betts, digging for information, so I said nothing and hoped he would offer to tell me about it. He didn't. It was starting to look as though Greg and his father had something to hide, the way he kept things to himself.

"So, about that tree, Shelby. What do you think? Is there a sound when it falls if no one is there to hear it?"

"I guess so." I felt like I'd been trapped into a trick question and he was going to tell me I was wrong.

"Why do you think so?"

"Well, because there is always sound when a tree falls, I guess. How could there be no sound? Just because no one hears it, that doesn't mean it isn't there." I was warming to the question.

"I think scholars believe there's no sound," Greg said, looking puzzled at the idea. "It seems that a person is supposed to think their way through to that idea. I have to admit though, I could never see it that way either. What you're saying makes sense to me, and yet I think there's more to it than what seems obvious."

"In science class one time we did an experiment with an alarm clock and a jar," I said, trying to remember the details. "If you pump all the air out of the jar, you can't hear the clock ringing because sound can't exist in a vacuum. I guess that's a different thing though, isn't it?"

Before he could answer, Nick passed by the table. When he did, he stopped for a few seconds and said, "Hi, Shelby."

My stomach did flip-flops all over the place. I tried to sound calm when I answered, "Hi, Nick," but my voice was trembling.

Greg looked hard at me after Nick had left. I guess he saw something on my face that he didn't like, because he was silent after that. I was too, because I was angry that he was sitting there when Nick finally spoke to me. He was going to ruin my chances with Nick if he didn't leave me alone.

He finished his lunch and stood, picking up his wrappers and brushing crumbs off the table.

"Well, I'll see you later then."

"Yeah, see you." I was thankful he was leaving. Maybe Nick would come back and want to talk to me.

"Enjoy the books," he added quietly and then left the cafeteria.

I stayed put right until the bell rang, just in case Nick came by again, but he didn't.

Chapter Four

The first fire happened during the second week of school, and the talk swung around to take it in. Everyone had a bit of information to share, and there were important comments made all over Little River High.

It was the Brennans' barn that burned, erupting into flames in the middle of the night. The fire marshal decided that it must have been caused by one of the cigars Mr. Brennan was forever smoking. Mr. Brennan hotly denied that he ever smoked in the barn, but he was getting on in years, and the townsfolk figured he'd done it without even realizing it. Stories about Mr. Brennan's forgetfulness got told over and over, as though that proved everything.

Then, only four days later, the shed out behind the Martins' house burned down. People might have started to wonder right then and there if something was afoot, seeing as how Little River hardly ever has a fire, and two in one week was pretty odd. But Mrs. Martin offered up the culprit.

"If I told Billy once, I told him a thousand times not to leave those rags and paint supplies out there. I knew this was going to happen someday," she told the fire marshal. It seemed a reasonable explanation, and the two fires coming so close together was soon chalked up to coincidence.

So Mr. Martin took the blame. From what I've heard, that's generally the way things go in the Martin house anyway.

Just as the talk of the fires was dying down, the third fire occurred. This time it was the Fennetys' house, which was completely destroyed. It didn't take much for the fire marshal to discover that it had been set deliberately. An empty gasoline can was found in the lot next door, and other evidence proved arson was the cause.

Betts brought a newspaper clipping about the story to school, and I felt sad reading Mr. Fennety's comments.

"Thank goodness my wife and little boy were visiting at her mother's place for a few days, or this tragedy could have been a lot worse. As it is, we lost everything we had." The story went on to say that the Fennetys had some insurance but that it was not nearly enough to replace the house. Theirs had been one of the older homes in the town, a huge two-storey building that had been passed down through several generations. I couldn't help thinking what a shame it was that it had been destroyed and wondering what kind of person would do such a thing.

The town rallied, as it always does when something happens to one of its own. A hootenanny was held, clothing and furniture were donated, and the bank set up an account for anyone who wanted to give the unfortunate family money.

The really sad thing about it all was the change in Mrs. Fennety. Before the fire, she'd been a cheerful and talkative person. After the fire, there was such a profound change in her that you'd have thought it was a completely different woman. She became withdrawn and had a worried, pinched look on her face all the time.

It was understandable that she'd be afraid, considering that someone had burned her house to the ground. She must have wondered if they'd thought she was home at the time and had been trying to kill her.

The fourth and last fire of the fall happened two weeks after the Fennety house went. This time it was an abandoned farmhouse out at Parker Point.

The sight of smoke billowing in the air was starting to be frighteningly familiar to the people of Little River. A town meeting was held, and a lot of folks started demanding that the local police department call in some help.

Once again, Betts brought the newspaper account of the story for me to see. It featured a big picture of Police Chief Bob Kendel. Under the picture it said, "We are here to serve and protect, and serve and protect is what we will do." The story went on to say that the people of Little River could put their confidence in the officers, who were trained and able to handle the situation.

Still, the people of Little River would have kept right on worrying about it if it hadn't been for Officer Lambert's wife. A week into the investigation she swore two of her close friends to secrecy and then told them that there was a suspect in the case. I don't think it took too much prodding before she swore them to secrecy on the rest of the details. And of course, those two friends swore a few of their friends to secrecy and told them. That's the way things happen in Little River.

Before the sun had gone down, almost everyone in town had been sworn to secrecy and the whole town had heard the news. It was just too big to keep, and the people of Little River aren't what you'd call famous for keeping secrets anyway.

It was, you might have guessed, Betts who told me about it. She couldn't wait for school the next day and came bursting in the door of my house around seven o'clock in the evening. I figure she'd heard the news about five minutes before then, since it's a five minute walk from her house to mine.

"Shelby, Shelby, guess what!" she called out, running down the entrance hall into the kitchen where Mom and I were making peanut butter cookies.

"Hello, Betts," my mom said, looking a little miffed at the way she'd barreled into the house without so much as knocking on the door.

"Hi, Mrs. Belgarden," she said breathlessly and then turned her attention back to me. "Did you heard about Greg Taylor's father?"

"What about him?" I asked.

"He's the one — the fire starter!" Betts' hazel eyes shone with the news. "I told you there was something strange about him."

"Now, Betts, how do you know this?" My mother was wiping her hands on her apron, and her face had a set look that I couldn't quite figure out.

"Everyone knows by now," Betts said, as though that settled it. "I imagine they'll be arresting him any minute. You see ..."

But before she could finish what she was saying, Mom held her hand up in that way she has that looks like a little stop sign. Her face had turned cross. "Betts, this is not a matter to be gossiping about. A man's good name is being ruined on the basis of rumours. I believe that in this country a person is innocent until proven guilty, and I don't recall anything being proven here."

"Yes, but they have proof," Betts pouted, looking

like she thought she was about to be cheated out of telling the rest of the story. And she was right.

"In this house," my mother said firmly, "we do not talk about people like this. If Malcolm has done something wrong, then it can be proven in court. We won't be trying and convicting him under this roof."

"Mr. Taylor's first name is Malcolm?" I asked, surprised. "How do you know?"

"I met him at the library when they first moved here," Mom said simply. "He's a very nice man, and I don't think he's done anything wrong. But if he has, that isn't for us to decide."

Betts and I were both too astonished by that to say anything.

Since she could see she wasn't going to get to say anything more, Betts soon left, anxious to find someone else who hadn't yet heard the story.

After she'd gone, Mom took off her apron, folded it neatly, and then sat down at the table.

"I think we should talk about this, Shelby," she said quietly. "You're going to hear about it at school, and I think it would be better if you got an accurate account of what's going on, instead of the wild stories the people of this town tell."

I sat down and waited for her to continue.

"The first thing I want to say, Shelby, is that gossip is an awful thing. You already know how I feel about that.

The fires we've had here in the last month were terrible, but, in a way, the gossip is more damaging than the fires."

That's something I really admire about my mother. She always sees the whole picture.

"Anyway," she went on, "I met Malcolm Taylor, as I already told you, when he and Greg first came to town. I was at the library one afternoon, and we struck up a conversation. He and his son came here for two reasons. The first one is the cause of all this talk.

"Malcolm was a professor at a university. He, his wife, and their son were just living a normal life, until something happened that changed everything. Their house caught fire one night. Malcolm and his son got out, but his wife died in the fire.

"It was a horrible thing for them, losing her. Both Malcolm and Greg found it too hard to stay there, so he gave up his job and they moved to Little River."

"Is that why the police think he had something to do with the fires?" I asked, feeling sorry for Greg. I couldn't imagine what it would be like if anything happened to my mother.

"I suppose he could be considered a suspect because of that, if indeed he's under suspicion. It may be that the police are jumping to conclusions. But they have nothing to base the idea on except this unfortunate coincidence." Mom looked suddenly very tired, as though the effort of talking about it was too much for her.

"What's the other reason they came here?" I asked, remembering she'd said there were two.

"Part of the healing they need comes from being in a different place," she explained, "and the other part is finding a way to deal with it effectively. Malcolm is working on a book to help him get through the loss. Writing can be very therapeutic."

I found it hard to sleep that night. I kept thinking about all of the things that were happening and wondering how they all fit together. I also decided that I was going to make an effort to be nice to Greg, even though I knew the other kids at school would make it hard.

CHAPTER FIVE

Most of the people of Little River were pretty engrossed in the whole fire story thing for the next few weeks. The stories got stranger and stranger as time went by, and it was impossible not to hear them.

It's amazing how rumours grow over time, don't you think? Mom had told me about how this can happen, how people take a story and "improve" it so that when they tell it to the next person it's a little more interesting. You'd have thought that the idea that Mr. Taylor was setting fires would be enough for people to talk about, but the stories kept getting weirder and weirder.

The really strange thing was how the rumours branched off into completely different ideas. If they'd all been true, Greg's dad would have had to be half a dozen different people. There were stories about him being involved in organized crime and hiding from the law in Little River. I'm not sure how that supported the theory that he was setting fires. You'd have thought that a person hiding from the law would refrain from drawing attention to himself, making it unlikely that he'd go around burning places down.

Other stories said that he was wealthy and planning a takeover of the town by scaring everyone into selling their property cheap. There was never an explanation put forward for why he'd want to own Little River.

The most common stories, though, were the ones that claimed he was mentally deranged. There were several variations on that theme. Some folks said that he had killed his wife and had gone over the edge and become a pyromaniac. Others suggested that the fire that killed Mrs. Taylor had been accidental and that he had lost his mind with grief and started setting fires out of some twisted idea of revenge or guilt for not being able to save her.

I knew one thing — the stories couldn't possibly all be true. Whatever the truth was, it wasn't going to surface in all the gossip.

The one really significant thing was actually something that *didn't* happen. I guess that sounds strange, but when people are expecting something to take place and it doesn't, it can mean just as much as something that actually does happen, if you know what I mean.

Anyway, the thing that didn't happen was that Greg's father didn't get arrested. Oh, there were lots of stories of how he'd been hauled into the police station for questioning. Some said in the dead of night, others were equally certain he'd been "grilled" for a full day. Most people covered this discrepancy by saying he'd been questioned on more than one occasion.

People began insisting that he was guilty and that the police just couldn't prove it.

Greg would have needed to have his head buried in the sand to avoid hearing all the rumours. I was sure he knew what was being said, but there was no change in the way he acted or how he held himself walking around. Usually if someone is embarrassed they'll keep their head down a bit or try not to look anyone in the eye.

Not Greg. He went along just the same as before. I'd see him here and there, smiling and talking to the other kids as if everything was perfectly normal. I have to admit that I admired that a little, the way he refused to be cowed by the stories. I'd have wanted to crawl off somewhere and hide if I'd been in his position.

You could see it in the faces around him too, puzzlement and something bordering on annoyance. It was as if they had been cheated out of the reaction they expected and didn't quite know what to do about it. Really, there was nothing they could do. It wasn't as if anyone could come right out and say anything to his face.

In keeping with my plan to be nice to him, I made an effort to say hello whenever I passed him in the hall.

He must not have known how difficult it was for me to do that with everyone around already talking about us as if there were some sort of romance brewing. In any case, he didn't show any sign of appreciating it much. He'd just smile and answer as if he'd fully expected me to speak to him and would have been surprised if I hadn't.

It took some of the noble feeling out of it for me. After all, I was making a pretty large gesture of kindness by acknowledging him, and he was acting as if it were his due.

Having said that, I have to admit that I didn't exactly go overboard being nice to him. Even though I spoke to him, I did my best to avoid getting into any real conversations. He obviously caught on too, because after a week or two he answered me when I spoke to him but didn't make any effort to take it any further.

Betts was over her snit and we were eating together again. It's comical the way Betts sprawls across the lunch table any time there's big gossip. She starts out by leaning forward and ends up with her arms spread out over the table and her chin nearly stuck into her lunch.

She'd finally accepted that there was nothing to the story about me and Greg, although I know this was a disappointment to her. That wasn't because she necessarily wanted to see me dating him at that point, but I'm sure she must have figured I'd be in a good position to get information out of him if I were his girlfriend.

In Betts's mind, Malcolm Taylor had been tried and convicted, and all that remained was for it to be made official. I did my best to avoid talking about it with her, which was no small feat. As soon as she'd bring up the subject, I'd steer the conversation away by mentioning something about whichever guy was the Man of Her Dreams at the moment. That usually worked, although it was trying for me to have to listen to her rave on and on about the various guys' eyes and lips. When she progressed to how cute someone's butt was, I'd wish I'd just let her gossip about Mr. Taylor!

Well, as I mentioned before, there were no more fires that fall. After a while things settled back to normal and the talk of Greg's father died down, to be resurrected only when things were really boring. There'd been no arrest, and it began to appear that the culprit was going to get away with it. People were unhappy about that. It was a real disappointment to have that kind of excitement fizzle out without the expected drama of an arrest and trial.

Even a great story like the fires can't keep going when there's nothing new to feed it. By the time November had passed, the town's adults had switched to talking about the usual things. I've never understood why it's interesting to old folks, which I suppose would include anyone over twenty-five, to spend their time discussing really boring stuff. The women seem to talk mostly about who's getting married or having a baby, while the men generally spend all of their time trying to decide whether or not it's going to rain.

As for the kids at school, we were mainly talking about the upcoming school dance. We have one every year, a week or so before Christmas, and it's a really big deal. It's embarrassing if you don't have a date, but some people go alone anyway, just so they don't have to miss out on it. The girls start getting their dresses as early as September, shopping out of town in bigger cities, or sometimes ordering material from Della's Fabric Store on the town square and having them made.

My mom was making mine, a deep blue formal gown with a glittery sash. She insisted on fittings every time I turned around, but I didn't really mind because that just meant it was going to fit perfectly. Even when it wasn't done, I felt special with the soft, satiny material flowing down around me.

Naturally, I'd been hoping that Nick Jarvis would ask me to be his date. Well, by the first week of December there was no sense in pretending that was going to happen. He'd made it official with Jane Goodfellow by then and asked her out. Jane was telling everyone that her gown was going to make the others look like country frocks. Did I mention that I don't like Jane Goodfellow?

Still, there were a couple of other guys at school who would have been pretty acceptable dates, even if they weren't Nick. I waited and prayed and turned down a few offers, hoping that one of them might come through. By the week of the formal, it was clear that I'd made a big mistake. Everyone worth going with was taken, and there I was with a dress and no date.

I know it's no excuse for what I did next, but I was desperate.

You're probably thinking that I accepted a last-minute invitation from Greg, but it's way worse than that. You see, Greg didn't actually ask me. I'd been thinking he might, but he never brought it up.

What happened was that, in a moment of panic, *I* asked *him*. To say he looked surprised is an understatement. It must have been a shock all right, after the way I'd basically been avoiding him.

He was outside waiting for his bus, standing off to one side with a faraway look on his face. Greg is like that a lot. You can see that he's drifted away from whatever is going on around him, which I have to admit I do too sometimes.

I got looking at him and thinking that he really wasn't all that bad. He's not a geek or anything, and even though he's not exactly handsome, he's at least passable. All of a sudden he seemed like a reasonable solution to the dance problem. Actually, by that point in time, he was pretty much the *only* solution.

"If you're going to the dance, and you don't have a date, I was thinking maybe we could go together." I'd walked up beside him and blurted it out before I could change my mind.

His astonishment was evident, but he pushed it aside quickly.

"I hadn't been planning to go," he said quietly. "It's formal wear, isn't it?"

"Most of the guys are just wearing suits." I felt like a total idiot. It seemed almost as if I was begging him. "It's not like you need a tuxedo or anything."

"I guess I could find something."

He smiled then and agreed to go. It was obvious that he was happy about it, but I went home with mixed feelings. While I was relieved that I wouldn't be one of those girls who can't get a date, I also partly regretted that I'd opened my mouth.

CHAPTER SIX

I was as casual as possible when I told my mom that I was going to the dance with Greg, but it's darned near impossible to hide anything from her. The way her head snapped up as she looked at me made it clear that I was going to have some explaining to do. So when the first thing she did was ask *why* I was going to the formal with Greg, it didn't come as a surprise.

"It's just a date," I said sullenly. I was in for "a talk," and I knew it.

"Well, let's see." She got that look on her face, the one that says we're going to get to the bottom of this and there will be no worming out of it. "You've told me how he embarrassed you and how you've avoided him ever since. Now all of a sudden you're going to the school formal with him. Tell me what I'm missing here."

"He's not that bad." This sounded lame even to me.

"He's not that bad." Mom repeated my words in a way that made it sound like the most ridiculous statement in the entire world. "And you feel this is a good reason to date someone."

"I'm not dating him. It's just a dance."

There was an uncomfortable moment then. Well, uncomfortable for me. She sat looking at me as though she couldn't quite understand what I'd said, as though I'd asked her a really hard question and she was figuring it out.

"Shelby, are you going with Greg just so that you'll have a date for the formal?"

It was useless to deny it. She had me, and we both knew it.

"I guess. But it's not like I'm doing anything wrong," I insisted. "We'll both get to go and have a good time. He wasn't going to go at all otherwise."

"I'm afraid I disagree," Mom said with disappointment on her face. "You're treating someone's feelings carelessly, and that's always wrong."

"You'd rather see me go alone and feel like a moron and have a terrible time," I snapped back accusingly, even though I knew it wasn't fair or true. For some reason, I seem to get angry when my mother points out something that makes me feel guilty.

"That's quite enough of that kind of talk."

"I'm sorry," I mumbled half-heartedly, "but you don't know how it feels."

"Don't I? Are you sure about that?"

Here we go with the "I was young once too" stories, I thought. How can you compare the way things were years ago when my mom was young to how they are now? It doesn't make sense. The world has changed a lot since then.

"As a matter of fact, Shelby," Mom was indeed launching into the past, but at least it would take the interrogation light off me for a minute, "when I was just a few years older than you, there was a couples' picnic out at Hawks Point. Everyone was going, but I didn't have a date until the last minute."

"Did you ask a guy you really didn't like much just so you'd have someone to go with?" In spite of myself, I was getting interested in her story.

"No, I didn't. But I wasn't there very long before I realized that's exactly what my date had done. He wasn't the least bit interested in being there with me, which was clear by the way he left me standing by myself while he made a fool of himself over another girl."

I felt my face getting hot and wondered if I was blushing. Was it possible that Mom had seen through me? Could she have figured out that I'd secretly been hoping that once I was at the dance, in my elegant gown, Nick might notice me?

"You must have felt pretty bad," I said, drawing myself back to her story.

"Sure I did. I went home that night and cried myself to sleep. And it wasn't just because of the way he'd treated me, it was because his actions proved he was completely indifferent to how I felt. I just didn't matter."

That really got to me. I realized that I hadn't stopped, not even for a second, to think about Greg's feelings. He was a means to an end, a convenience. It wasn't a proud moment for me.

"Do you think I should call off the date with Greg?"

"I don't think that will make things a whole lot better, do you?"

"I guess not. What should I do then?"

"I'm sure you'll figure out the best thing to do." She smiled and patted my knee.

Letting me figure things out when I've made a mess of some sort is probably Mom's favourite form of torture. She points things out and makes me think until I'm all in a tangle inside, feeling guilty and confused, and then leaves me to decide how to get out of it.

Lots of times when I have to think something through I find it helps to take a long walk. I hauled my jacket back on and headed out, hoping that the whole thing would sort itself out in my head.

The sun was shining, making the early December snowfalls glisten so sharply that it could take your breath away. That kind of beauty usually cheered me, but it really didn't seem to help much that day. I knew the worst part of what I'd done was that Greg was going to get the wrong impression. For sure he'd assume I liked him; what else could he think? Undoing that would mean hurting his feelings, there was no way around it.

I wished I wasn't even going to the dance. At that moment I'd have gladly given up the beautiful dress Mom had made me if I could just take back the foolish invitation. But, like most mistakes, it was done and couldn't be undone. It's so much easier to get into a mess than out of it!

There was no easy answer, and it soon became clear to me that the only course of action for the time being was to go and be really nice to Greg. I hoped that he wouldn't expect it to lead to other dates, but I knew different.

I was on my way back home when I saw Betts's familiar face coming along the street. It looked as though she was heading towards The Scream Machine, but when she spied me she waved and hurried over.

"Hey Shelb, where you going? I just called your place, but you're not there."

That sounded funny, as if I didn't know I wasn't home. It made me smile in spite of my misery.

"Nowhere, really. Just walking."

"I was going to get an order of fries." She smiled as if she was really looking forward to that. I knew different. Half the time, Betts has to fend for herself at suppertime because her mom works two jobs. Her dad has a good job too, but they have a really fancy house and two new cars, and I guess they need a lot of money coming in to pay for everything.

I'm glad that my mom doesn't have to work, although sometimes she sells pictures to the local paper. My mom took up photography a few years back, and she's actually pretty good at it. She can capture a scene in a way that makes it really stand out. We have a dark-room downstairs now and it's really cool.

"Why don't you come to my place for supper instead?" I offered. "Mom made a big boiled dinner, so there'll be lots." Mom never minded me bringing some-one home for a meal.

"I think I'll just stick with fries," Betts answered. "Anyway, I think that Graham is going to be at The Scream Machine, and I want to remind him about a couple of things for the dance."

Graham was Betts' new boyfriend. He's a nice enough guy I guess, but not the hunk Betts made him sound like when she told me she was going out with him. He'd been hanging around her for a while, though she hadn't been interested in him at first. I guess he sort of grew on her.

I realized then that Betts didn't know I was going to the dance with Greg. I took a deep breath and told her.

"No way!" she squealed, getting all excited. I gave her a minute to calm down and stop waving her arms and doing this funny kind of spastic bounce she does when she gets animated.

"Oh, I knew it! I just knew it!" She hugged me then, a big squeeze that almost made me lose my balance when she let go. "I knew he liked you. Oh, this is perfect."

I laughed in spite of myself. It's nice to have a friend who's really happy when she thinks something good is happening to you, even though in this case she was wrong. Betts is loyal to the end, not like some girls who say stuff about their friends behind their backs.

"I'm just going to the dance with him, Betts," I tried to calm her. "It's not like some big romance or anything."

"We'll see." She smiled and giggled as if she knew a secret.

I didn't have the heart to burst her bubble, so I just let her think what she wanted to.

At least one of us was happy about my date with Greg.

CHAPTER SEVEN

"Wow! You look beautiful!"

Greg was standing in the living room, holding a pale blue wrist corsage in his hand. I'd just come in through the hall doorway, regretting that we didn't have a big circular staircase like you see in the movies. You know the scene, when the heroine comes floating down, pausing a couple of times while everyone watches her, awestruck.

Not that I think I'm glamorous or anything, but in a long dress, with my hair done up in a French braid, I felt like someone else altogether.

"Thanks." Greg looked nice too, in a black suit with a white shirt and burgundy tie. I was just about to say something about it when Mom spoke up.

"Doesn't your date look handsome in his suit, dear?"

It made me mad that she'd butted in.

"You look great," I told him, but it must have seemed as if I was just agreeing with Mom. Maybe he thought I was just saying it because I had to, because she'd trapped me into it with her question.

He seemed happy anyway, although a bit embarrassed by the compliment.

"What a lovely corsage," Mom broke in again.

"Oh, yeah," Greg looked startled, and I figured he'd forgotten about the flower in his hand. "This is for you." He slid it onto my wrist. It really was pretty, a cluster of tiny pale blue flowers among sprigs of white baby's breath.

"Sorry, they had no orchids left."

I assured him it was beautiful and thanked him while Mom hovered around us making comments. I tried to give her a hint that her interference wasn't wanted, but if she noticed the covert frowns and glares she managed to ignore them completely.

"Well, I guess we'd better be going," I said in desperation. Where was Dad anyway? He was supposed to drive us to the school, but he was nowhere to be seen.

"Go?" Mom cried, as though I'd just proposed killing someone. "Not before I get some pictures you won't!" She ran off to get her camera.

I felt as though I was trapped in some sort of pre-dance torture chamber from which there might never be an escape.

"Sorry." I rolled my eyes while looking at Greg. "She's not usually this weird."

"I think she's sweet. I wish … "

His voice trailed off without finishing the sentence, but it wasn't hard to figure out what he'd been about to say. It hit me with a jolt that his mother was dead and that he'd probably give anything to have her there fussing over us and taking pictures.

"Oh, Greg. I wasn't thinking. I didn't mean …" It was my turn to be unable to go on.

"It's okay," he said, "it's easy to forget how lucky we are sometimes and to take people for granted."

I have to say that I was able to tolerate the picture taking session without being annoyed after that. Even though Mom was still flitting around and saying embarrassing things, it didn't bother me any more. I even told Greg that she'd made my dress and didn't mind that she tittered and giggled when he complimented her on it.

It seemed that Mom was more excited about the dance than I was. But then, she didn't have any guilt to deal with, and I did.

I was just about to start fretting again when Dad arrived at last, apologizing for the delay. He explained that he'd gone to have the car cleaned.

"A man has to take his chauffeur duties seriously," he said jocularly, then broke off and stared at me. "My, my," he sounded all choked up, "just look at you."

After he'd stammered a few comments about me being "all grown up" and told me how nice I looked, we finally headed out, arriving at the same time as some other couples were entering the school. The auditorium was decorated with streamers and balloons and what looked like thousands of flowers made from coloured tissue. It had been transformed into a fairyland. The lights were covered in crepe paper, which gave the room a soft blue or purple glow, depending on where you were standing.

I was trying to keep the butterflies in my stomach under control, but it was my first formal dance and I had started to get flutters as soon as we walked in. I saw Betts across the room, and she beckoned us over to where she and Graham were standing.

We made our way through the growing crowd, pausing every few feet to say hello to other kids. Most of the guys looked kind of sheepish in their suits, but the girls were all squealing in admiration over each other's dresses. Of course, as soon as someone complimented someone else's dress, the other person gushed the same thing back, each insisting that the other dress was nicer. I looked around for Jane, wondering if her dress was going to be the big hit she'd claimed, but she was nowhere to be seen.

Then I saw Nick, standing with a couple of other guys. I figured Jane was in the girls' room, probably fixing her lipstick or, I thought unkindly, maybe just looking in the mirror. I'd seen her doing that before, just staring at herself as though she couldn't tear herself away from her own reflection.

Annie Berkley was there with Todd Saunders. They're both in my class, and it was quite a surprise when we found out Todd was taking Annie to the dance. Todd is a good-looking guy and quite popular, but Annie is chubby and has curly hair that always seems to want to fly in the wrong directions. She has a nice smile and is friendly and all, but she's no beauty. No one could figure out why he'd asked her.

Annie's dress was the worst possible design for her figure. It was pale yellow, tied at the waist with a wide sash that made the rest of the fabric bulge out around it. Big balloon-style sleeves puffed out over her shoulders like oversized football pads. Instead of flattering her figure, it made her look twice her actual size.

Naturally I told her the dress was beautiful. She thanked me with her eyes averted and then quickly added that mine was very pretty too, though I don't see how she could tell since she wasn't exactly looking at me. I felt really bad, because I could see how uncomfortable she was and how out-of-place and awkward she was feeling in her big puffy dress. She looked as if she'd rather be anywhere but at the dance.

We moved on then, Greg and I, making our way through the crowd. I was keeping an eye out for Jane but still hadn't seen her by the time we finally reached Betts and Graham.

Betts was in high form to say the least! She was giggling and talking to three or four people at once, tossing out remarks and turning from person to person, her face lit up and glowing with excitement. She squealed and hugged me when we got there.

"Oh, isn't this just the best! I can't wait until the band goes on stage. Oh! Your dress is perfect! Mine is too severe I think. I should have gone with the mauve one Mom wanted me to get, but this one was just so divine on the model."

I'd already seen Betts in her sleek black dress about twenty times and had told her every time that it was great. I was just about to repeat the assurance I'd given on those occasions when Greg spoke up.

"I wouldn't call it severe. Actually, it's very elegant."

"Oh, Greg, you're such a sweetie!" Betts gushed. "Do you really think so?"

He smiled and nodded but said nothing else. I figured that he'd used up all his ability to pay a compliment with that one remark. Guys aren't exactly good at offering commentaries on women's clothes!

"And Graham, isn't Shelby's dress to die for?"

Graham laughed at Betts's enthusiasm, took a deep bow, and told me with considerable exaggeration that my dress was divine. I curtsied back and told him he was dashing and debonair in his suit.

"Oh, poor Greg," Graham said then in a falsetto voice that made him sound exactly like a girl. "You must be feeling left out."

"Yes, you must Greg," Betts added, giggling at Graham's female voice. "But you look really yummy!"

"That's exactly what I was thinking earlier when I saw myself in the mirror," he said deadpan. "I couldn't help noticing how yummy I was. Thanks for mentioning it, Betts."

The band came on then, playing a hard, driving tune. Once the first few brave couples hit the dance floor almost everyone else rushed over to join them. I saw Nick dancing with Kelsey Princeton, who had left her date standing in the corner looking dejected. Nick glanced my way a few times, and it made me feel really awkward. I'm not a very good dancer anyway, but then I haven't had much practice.

It wasn't long before I found out why Nick wasn't dancing with Jane. Betts cleared it up for me when the band took its first break.

"Did you hear about poor Jane?" she gasped, out of breath from the last dance. "She took a dizzy spell and fell and hurt herself."

"What a shame." I tried to put something that sounded like sympathy into my voice, but all I could feel was disappointment. Because of my own stupidity,

I was stuck with Greg for the evening. There was Nick without a partner, and I was going to miss out on the chance to dance with him.

Then something else happened that almost spoiled the evening for everyone. The fire alarm sounded, screaming over the music. We all hurried outside the way we always do when there's a drill, but we knew they'd never have a drill during a dance.

We stood shivering in the cold for about ten minutes before one of the teachers came out and told us we could return to the auditorium. Once inside, an explanation was given, and we learned that there had been a fire in the wastebasket of the girls' washroom.

"This is very serious," the teacher said sternly. "I assume that someone was smoking in the washroom and threw the cigarette butt in the garbage without properly extinguishing it. You all know that there is no smoking permitted in this building. If I so much as smell a hint of smoke anywhere in this school again this evening, the dance will end immediately."

There were no further incidents, but after all the other fires we'd had through the fall I couldn't help wondering if it had really been accidental. Still, we were all having a good time, and it didn't make sense that anyone would deliberately ruin the dance.

CHAPTER EIGHT

In spite of everything else, it turned out that the dance was awesome. In fact, I was still walking on air the next Monday morning when I got to school. Even though I hadn't been able to dance with Nick, what happened was the next best thing. The high point came when I was standing alone while Greg went to bring us back some raspberry punch from the tables along the wall.

"Having a good time?"

I turned to see Nick standing to my left with this incredibly adorable smile on his face. He was leaning toward me a little, and I could smell cologne on him.

"Yes, thanks," I managed to stammer, then thought to add, "Sorry to hear about Jane."

"Yeah, well," he shrugged, "what can you do?"

"I guess."

"I'd really like to dance with you. Think Greg would mind?" He winked, and my stomach flip-flopped all over the place. I frantically hoped I wasn't turning red.

I wanted to tell him that I'd love to dance with him, but my throat had constricted and I couldn't get any words out right away. I pictured what it would be like to have his arms around me, my face pressed to his shoulder. If I'd had another minute I might have found my voice, so it's probably lucky that Greg came back then and saved me from my own weakness. I'd promised myself I'd do the right thing and be really nice to Greg while I was his date, and there I'd been, on the verge of breaking my promise.

"Hey, Nick."

"Greg, you lucky dog. You've got yourself quite a babe here tonight."

If Greg answered him, I sure didn't hear it. Nick thought I was quite a babe! His words echoed in my head for the rest of the night and on through the weekend.

There was no doubt in my mind that Nick was going to ditch Jane and ask me out. I played the scene over and over in my head, how he'd call me up or maybe come right up to me at school and tell me he was through with her, that it was me he wanted. In my imaginings, I accepted him with grace and poise. I blocked out the fact that the few short conversations I'd ever had with Nick had left me blushing and tongue-tied.

But at lunch on Monday he was sitting with Jane as usual, touching her hands and smiling. My only consolation was that she looked awful from when she'd had the dizzy spell and fallen. There was a dark bruise on her cheek, and though she'd obviously tried to cover it with makeup, I could still see the shadow from across the cafeteria.

Of course I realized then that he couldn't just up and dump her after she'd hurt herself and missed the dance and all. Obviously he was waiting for the right time. But there was only another day and a half of school before the winter break. It was clear that I was going to have to bide my time.

I was just congratulating myself on my patient and mature attitude when Greg slid in beside me at the table. Betts was having lunch with Graham and I could have joined them, but you know what that would be like. I'd have felt like an outsider — watching them smile at each other and hearing everything they said.

"Hey," Greg greeted me. He looked happy.

"Hi," I answered without enthusiasm. I silently willed him away.

"I was wondering if maybe you'd like to take in a movie over the holidays."

"Uh, I don't know. I'm going to be pretty busy with family plans and stuff."

"Ah, a full social calendar. You must be very much in demand. Perhaps I should call your secretary to make an appointment."

I smiled at that, feeling foolish. Greg wasn't dumb enough to think I had no time for a movie over a whole two weeks off school.

"I meant, it would depend on when you wanted to go," I said, figuring I could always put him off when he tried to pin me down for a specific time.

"This may be a challenge, what with your full schedule and my shifts at work. But I think we can overcome these formidable obstacles. If we want to." He had a look on his face that was both serious and teasing at the same time.

Why did he have to talk like that? Formidable obstacles, for goodness' sake! He sounded like some character in a book, not a normal teen having a normal conversation. I glanced around, hoping no one had heard.

"Yes, I suppose we could. If we want to." I put the same emphasis on "if we want to" that he had when he'd said it. Maybe he'd take the hint.

Across the room, Nick was laughing at something Jane had just said. I'd never found Jane to be much of a wit myself. He was probably being polite.

"You know, Shelby, nothing makes a girl more attractive to a guy than the fact that another guy is interested in her."

"Huh?" I thought I must have missed something between the last thing we were saying and this remark. It seemed to come out of nowhere.

"For example, let's just say hypothetically that there was a couple sitting here in the lunchroom and that the female half of the couple was rather taken with someone else. So she's half listening to the fellow at her table, but following every move made by the other guy, who, for example, could be sitting across the room with another girl."

I felt myself getting red. He hadn't missed my glances at Nick, which I thought were pretty well hidden.

"Forget for the moment whether the other guy is suited to this young lady, or whether her affection for him is a shocking display of bad taste. Ignoring the fact that he is all wrong for her, let us say that her heart is firmly set on him."

"This is ridiculous."

"Is it? But Shelby, we are only speaking hypothetically, remember?"

"Then get to your hypothetical point. You're starting to aggravate me."

"Excellent. I'd begun to think myself incapable of evoking any emotion from you whatsoever. But I digress. Returning to our situation, let us examine what the best course of action would be for our heroine to obtain the affections of the undeserving cad who has mysteriously captured her heart."

I have to admit I was starting to enjoy the way he was talking. It was different and fun and interesting to listen to the way he said things.

"This delightful young woman, who so foolishly desires the wrong fellow, has but one chance of securing his interest."

"And what would that be?"

"Why, she must be sought after, longed for, by another. This will make her more desirable to the unworthy fellow she imagines herself smitten with."

"And how does she manage this?"

"Why, by seeming to accept the attentions of the fellow at her side. By showing interest in him, even if she is only playing at it."

"And what advantage is that to him, since she's not really interested in him at all?" This may have been a bit cruel, but he'd said enough embarrassing things about me that it seemed only fair for me to take a shot back at him.

"His advantage is that he then has the chance, however slim, to open her eyes."

"Meaning what?"

"That perhaps, just perhaps, she will realize that he is the right one for her after all."

"And if that doesn't happen?"

"Then they must both pay the price for her folly. It's a risk he would be prepared to take."

Folly indeed! As if he knew anything about Nick. As if I was ever going to think Greg would make a better boyfriend than Nick would. It was ridiculous.

It was also intriguing, the idea that he was willing to put himself in the position he'd just described. I could suddenly see the very real possibility that it would indeed help me get Nick's interest.

And I knew what Mom would have to say about such a thing. Not that I would ever discuss it with her, but in spite of that, her voice was in the back of my head pestering my conscience. I wonder sometimes how she manages to come through at moments like that. I'd just had a pretty tempting offer, and I couldn't take advantage of it because her unspoken disapproval hung over me like some sort of weird ethical cloud.

"Well, thanks for the fairy tale," I told Greg, standing up. "But if you ask me, it's the guy in your hypothetical story who needs his eyes opened, not the girl."

"You could be right," he smiled. "Maybe we can discuss it further at Christmas."

"Christmas?"

"Yes, your mother has kindly invited my dad and me to have Christmas dinner with your family."

I knew right off that he wasn't making that up. It

was just the kind of thing my mom would do. At that moment I wished she wasn't such a nice person!

Later on though, when I'd had more time to think about it, I decided that it wasn't really all that bad. Talking to Greg could be fun, especially if there was no one else nearby to hear some of the strange things he said. I figured I could stand having him around for a couple of hours. I was curious about his dad too, and this would be a chance to meet him.

Maybe I could look at him and somehow be able to tell if he was the Little River fire starter!

CHAPTER NINE

My stomach was growling from the smells of Christmas dinner by the time our family and the Taylors sat down to eat. Dad carved the turkey while steam wafted up from the dishes holding potatoes, gravy, stuffing, carrots, turnip, and warm rolls.

Greg and his father hadn't been at our place long when I saw where Greg got his way of talking. Mr. Taylor spun out conversation that captured our attention and held us still, waiting for more. It made me think of a spider's web.

He didn't look at all as I'd pictured him. In my imagination he'd been tall and thin and pale, with a beard and glasses. It had been a surprise to find that he was broad shouldered, with muscular forearms that bulged against the rolled-up sleeves of the blue plaid shirt he wore. His hair was long, about shoulder length, and looked as though he didn't give it much attention. It wasn't exactly messy; it just didn't have that overly styled look you usually see on an older guy who has long hair. There was no beard, no glasses, and he had a healthy, weathered look that you'd expect from someone who spends most of his time outdoors.

I liked him. When he spoke, he included everyone instead of passing over us teens and concentrating on the adults, like most grown-ups tend to do.

He didn't ask me how old I was or what grade I was in or how I liked school. Those questions irritate me. It's as though they're the only things adults can think of to ask a kid, and you can always tell they aren't really interested in your answers.

"Greg tells me that you have a love for literature, Shelby," he'd said during a break in the conversation. "Suppose that you were to spend five years in an isolated place, say a cabin in the woods where you'd have no contact with anyone. Suppose that you could take only three books with you."

"That's not very many," I said, dismayed at the thought. I couldn't imagine being limited to the same three books for five years.

"Then you'd have to choose very carefully."

"We have a book that contains the complete works of Shakespeare," my mom remarked. "Would it be cheating to take that?"

70

"Not at all, but this is Shelby's list."

"I hate Shakespeare," I moaned, "it's so hard to know what he's saying most of the time."

"I felt that way right through university," Mr. Taylor smiled. "It's a lot of work to read the Bard. You have to be willing to invest yourself in his writing."

I'd never thought of investing myself when I was reading anything. It was interesting to think of it in that way. It implied that there was a payoff for the effort.

"I really don't know what three I'd take," I said finally. I felt a little pressured, as though I was taking a test and hadn't been able to study for it.

"Excellent!" He lifted his empty fork up in the air as though he was holding up a scepter.

His proclamation startled me.

"That proves that you would choose well. You aren't willing to just name any three books you like. You'd want time to think it through, to make your selections with care."

I felt suddenly proud, as though I'd made perfect choices instead of saying I didn't know. And I felt as though my opinion was valued and interesting.

"Well, my first choice wouldn't take much thought," my dad spoke up. "I'd darned sure need a cookbook of some sort." He patted his stomach in satisfaction at the huge meal we'd all just shared. "Otherwise I'd be living on toast."

The subject of spending five years learning to survive and do everything for yourself spread out in front of us and kept us occupied through dessert. It was fun thinking of how you'd have to take provisions like flour and sugar and yeast to make bread and how you'd have to learn to scavenge off the land for some of your supplies.

"I couldn't trap poor innocent animals!" I said when the talk turned to procuring meat.

"What would you do for protein then?" Greg asked.

"I'd take peanut butter, and chickens for eggs."

"But your chickens have died and the peanut butter turned rancid."

"I'm not killing and skinning animals," I insisted, making a face at the thought. "There must be other things a person can get protein from."

"Perhaps you'd cook dried beans and our national food — oatmeal," Mr. Taylor offered helpfully.

I hadn't known that oatmeal contained protein or that it was Canada's national food. That seemed kind of funny until Mr. Taylor explained what a great food it actually is.

It was amazing how I learned so many things over dinner that day just by talking about stuff that was fun and interesting. I couldn't help but think that Mr. Taylor must have been a great teacher at college, the way he could get a person drawn into a topic and considering all different things about it.

All in all, it was a great meal. Well, except for one thing. When we were nearly finished eating, Mom went to get more coffee, and Dad followed her into the doorway where a sprig of mistletoe was hanging. To my horror, he kissed her right in front of everyone. Talk about gross! I made no effort to hide my disgust at this outrageous spectacle, but no one else seemed to mind it.

When we had stuffed mincemeat pie into our already full stomachs, our guests insisted on doing the dishes. Mom tried to object, but it was obvious she wasn't going to win, especially when Mr. Taylor said he'd arm wrestle her to see if he'd get his way.

Mom looked so surprised at the suggestion that we all laughed, and then she declined the arm wrestle and sent me off to the kitchen with them to show them where everything went.

I felt strangely proud of Mr. Taylor for doing this. It was such a nice way of repaying Mom for the dinner invitation. Even though she'd tried to refuse the offer, I knew she was tired from cooking all day long. It was great for her to be able to sit down in the living room and relax instead of having to do the big clean-up. And of course, I would have been helping her, so it was beneficial to me too.

It was kind of sad though, watching Greg and his dad doing the dishes. Mr. Taylor washed and Greg dried, and I couldn't help thinking about how they must do this together at home all the time because there was no Mrs. Taylor anymore. It looked wrong somehow, because she was missing from the picture. I wondered what she had looked like and how she had fit with the two of them.

Just as we were finishing up, Betts arrived to tell me about some of the gifts she'd received. I had a bad moment when she was introduced to Greg's dad and she got an excited look on her face. I thought for sure that she was going to start asking him embarrassing questions. It reminded me of how I'd been planning to watch him for signs that he might be the Little River fire starter, which by then struck me as ridiculous. There was no way a nice man like Mr. Taylor was involved in something like that.

I never found out whether or not Betts might have gotten around to prying because Greg suggested that the three of us go outside and build a snow sculpture.

"It's kind of dark out," Betts pointed out. She didn't seem that enthusiastic, but I was glad for the idea. After being in the hot kitchen, the thought of fresh air was more than welcome.

"We'll put on the porch light," I said, hauling on my jacket and gloves. "It'll be fun."

She shrugged and came along just as I knew she would. Betts is really a good sport, and even if she complains sometimes she always comes through.

We couldn't agree right away on what we were going to make so we just started making a big mound, building up a pile of snow in the middle of the yard. By the time we had enough to shape into a sculpture, we'd agreed on making a snow castle. It was just taking form when Betts tossed the first snowball and hit Greg on the arm.

"I can see that we're going to need to build a dungeon in our castle for this miscreant," he laughed, lobbing a snowball back at her.

"What did you call me?" she demanded, ducking and laughing.

"Thou art a most sneaky and evil villain," he said solemnly, gathering more snow into a ball.

Well, that was the end of our sculpture. Fluffy white orbs flew back and forth faster and faster until we were all out of breath and gasping with laughter. Our faces were red when we finally went back inside to warm ourselves. Greg's mitts were covered in snow and I banged them over the kitchen sink to knock some of it off before hanging them up to dry.

"Neat mitts," I commented. They were black with a red and purple design. He told me that it was an Aztec pattern and then added that his father had knitted them.

"Your dad knits!" Betts almost choked on the words.

"Yeah, why not?"

"Well, guys don't knit."

"And why is that?"

"Knitting is for women."

"Women have been fighting that very attitude for years. Do you think that men and women have to be restricted to certain roles?"

"That's not what she meant," I said quickly. I could see Betts's face clouding over, and I knew she wasn't going to win an argument with Greg.

"Don't you think Betts should speak for herself?"

"Come on, don't make a big deal over something this small."

"Stereotyping isn't a small thing. Men and women need to accept each other's right to make choices based on individuality, with all gender bias aside. Until that happens we're all affected by unfair restrictions and ideas."

Well, by then Betts was getting pretty upset. She left almost immediately, saying she'd call me the next day.

I was furious with Greg and hardly spoke to him again before he and his dad left. The nerve of him, coming to my house and starting a fight with my best friend!

On the other hand, I figured it was just the excuse I needed to avoid any more contact with him.

CHAPTER TEN

By the time school went back in, Betts seemed to have forgotten all about the argument she'd had with Greg. Well, maybe argument isn't exactly the right word. It's not as if she was holding up her side of it, and I think that's what bothered me the most. He knew perfectly well that she couldn't defend herself, especially since she didn't even know the meaning of some of the words he used. It was an unfair attack.

But Betts never holds a grudge for long, which is something I usually admire in her a lot. I can be way more stubborn and vindictive than she can, and her good nature has saved us from serious quarrels more than once.

Greg hadn't called me after Christmas, and I knew he was well aware that I wasn't too happy with him. I naturally assumed that was going to be the end of the whole matter with him.

So when Betts kept talking to me about him, how much he liked me and all that stuff, it was really exasperating. I did my best to point out how rude he'd been to her, but she laughed it off as if it wasn't worth remembering.

I guess that's where we first came in. Betts and her campaign to help me see that Greg was the Man of My Dreams. I think it was probably because she was still seeing Graham and wanted us both to have steady boyfriends so we could do things together as couples. Whatever her reason, it was wearing pretty thin, and I was just barely managing to stay patient about the whole thing.

Another big reason I needed to stay as far away from Greg as possible was that Nick had broken up with Jane. I saw her in the hallway the first day of school after the Christmas break and I almost felt sorry for her. She seemed really sad, walking with her eyes cast down and her face set hard and tight, as though she had something clenched between her teeth. It made me feel guilty when I thought of how happy I'd been to hear the news about their breakup.

"Nick got fed up having a girlfriend who never wants to go anywhere or do anything," Betts gave me the lowdown. "I heard that every time he called her to make plans she had some excuse that she couldn't go out."

That seemed strange all right, but then Jane has been kind of odd ever since I've known her. Her mom and dad divorced when she was little, and her mom remarried not too long afterward. I always figured that she never got over her folks splitting up like that. Still, I think her stepdad is okay. I remember seeing him walking with her when she was small, holding her hand and talking to her. Lots of dads don't spend as much time with their daughters as Jane's stepfather does with her.

Even these days it's common to see them driving along together. She's always leaning away from him, staring hard out the passenger window with a look of resentment on her face. And her attitude hasn't escaped people's notice either. I've heard more than one person talking about how spoiled and mean she acts, and what a nice man he is to keep making an effort to be a good father to her in spite of it.

Maybe it's natural for her to dislike him, since her own father isn't around anymore. Some kids never get over their folks splitting up and keep hoping that someday they'll get back together. I guess it's like that for Jane.

Well, I wasn't about to spend my time feeling sorry for Jane Goodfellow. She had her chance with Nick and she blew it. Now it would be someone else's turn, and I was determined that it was going to be me. Only I would be an ideal girlfriend, and he'd never want to break up with me.

By the time we'd been back in school for a week I was pretty confident that Nick was going to ask me out.

He went out of his way to talk to me and always gave me little hints that told me he was interested.

Then today on my way to history class he had just passed me in the hallway when he turned and called out, "Hey, Shelby."

I stopped in mid-step with the usual thrill running through me. Still, when I spun around to face him I did my best not to look too eager.

"Oh, hi Nick," I said, as if I hadn't noticed him walking by only seconds before.

"Are you doing anything tonight?"

My heart leapt right up into my throat. Well, I guess it didn't, but it sure felt like something was there. The best I could do was shake my head "no."

"Can you come over to my place later?" He reached his hand out and touched my arm in the most casual way, as if he didn't even notice he was doing it. His eyes looked right into mine. "You're a whiz at English, and I need some help with a stupid essay we have to write. I can't get anywhere with it, and it's due tomorrow."

"How much do you have done?" I managed to ask. I had a lot of homework of my own and a project in science that I'd sort of let slide for too long.

He smiled and shrugged in the most adorable way. "None actually. And the coach is going to suspend me from the basketball team if I don't bring my marks up. I could sure use your help."

I hesitated. If I didn't get my science project finished, I'd lose points for it being late. I really needed most of the evening to finish it and get the rest of my homework done.

"You said you weren't doing anything," he pointed out with another smile. "But if you can't make it, don't worry about it. I think Allison would probably give me a hand."

Allison! That conniving witch has been throwing herself at Nick forever. I could just picture her using the excuse to sit really close to him, batting her eyes and giggling. The thought almost made me sick.

"No, it's no problem. What time did you want me to come over?"

"Right after supper." His hand trailed down my arm and squeezed lightly before he took it away. "I'll be waiting."

After he left, I thought for sure I was going to be late for my next class. My knees were so weak I could hardly move, making it impossible to hurry down the hallway. I just got there and slid into my seat as the teacher was standing up to take attendance.

Mr. Rittner was up there talking on and on about Hannibal and elephants and some pass, but I really didn't hear much of what he was saying. There was something about a battle, but if anyone had asked me after class which side had won I couldn't have answered.

Thoughts of spending time alone with Nick raced through my head. He could have asked anyone to help him, but he'd chosen me! I knew it was just a matter of time before Nick Jarvis and I would be a couple. I'd be the envy of half the girls at Little River High.

Once home, I raced through some of my homework and then hardly touched my supper because my stomach was all tied up in nervous, excited knots. As soon as the kitchen was cleaned up I headed off to Nick's place.

He met me at the door with one of his adorable smiles and led me to the kitchen table where his books were piled.

"Sorry about the mess," he laughed. "My stuff isn't all that organized, but I'm sure you can find what you need." He flipped through a couple of binders and pulled out an assignment sheet.

"Here we go." He passed it to me and then fumbled through his stuff for a pen and some blank paper. When he gave me the pen his fingers brushed against mine ever so softly, sending a jolt up my arm.

I read the assignment and was a little dismayed that the essay had to be a thousand words long. It would take all evening, even if we hurried. I'd have to stay up half the night to get my science project finished. Well, it would be worth it!

"You're such a sweetheart."

A quiver went all through me when he said that, but it disappeared fast at his next words.

"I wish I could be here the whole time, but the team has a practice at seven." Seeing my dismayed look he added quickly, "Don't worry. It's a short one. I'll be home by eight or so."

His mom came into the room just then and looked quizzically at him.

"This is Shelby, Ma. Isn't she a babe? She's giving me a hand with an essay, so keep the TV down will you?" Then he tossed on his jacket and headed out the door.

I could hardly believe it. Instead of being alone with Nick, there I was, alone with his mom. It wasn't exactly how I'd pictured it!

I reminded myself that he'd be back in an hour and got to work. Before long I was concentrating hard on the essay and trying not to watch the clock too closely. Still, I couldn't help but notice when eight-thirty passed and he still wasn't back. Then it was nine, and nine-thirty. At ten minutes to ten I had the essay finished.

There was nothing left to do then but tell his mother goodnight and leave.

CHAPTER ELEVEN

On the walk home I was trying to think of excuses for Nick not coming back to his house. Everything I came up with sounded lame, and my disappointment was turning to anger. Well, anger and humiliation. And since I'd let it happen, I wasn't sure if I was angry at Nick or at myself.

Before very long though, something happened that completely erased all thoughts of Nick Jarvis from my mind. Well, for the moment anyway. Something was wrong.

When I first smelled smoke in the air I'd assumed it was just someone's wood furnace, but then I realized it was too thick, and it didn't have the right smell.

Even though it was dark, it didn't take long to discover the source of the fire. As I was passing a house I could see an orange glow, like the beginning of a sunrise, on the next street over. After all the fires in the early fall, it gave me a creepy feeling, but I was curious too. I rounded the corner and hurried toward it. At the same time I could hear sirens in the distance.

I got there just before the fire truck raced to the blazing building. It was the Lawfords' big double garage that was burning. The first thing I noticed was that the doors were open and there were no cars inside. The house was dark and quiet too, and I figured the family was out for the evening. I wondered what would have happened if there had been a car in there when the fire started, if the gas tank would have blown up or not.

I stood back when the firemen leapt from the truck and fastened hoses to a nearby fire hydrant. They were amazingly fast, and it seemed that only seconds passed from the time they got there until powerful streams of water were pulsing into the flames.

People were gathering on the sidewalk, and even in the dark you could see that their expressions were grim and anxious. I backed away a little more, watching the crowd and wondering if the person who'd set the fire was in its midst.

Thankfully, the firefighters got the blaze out before it spread to any other buildings. The police were there by then too, and were keeping everyone back away from the scene. I knew they had to make sure that no one disturbed any evidence that was there. No one seemed inclined to leave though, they just hung back and watched, even though the fire was out and all that was left to see was a soggy mess of charred wood and smouldering debris.

Walking away, I couldn't help but think that it was starting again! My stomach felt sick thinking of how the town was going to react, how the gossip would rise up again and swallow the truth, how people would feel afraid not knowing where the fire starter might strike next. My steps were slow as I considered these things, which is probably the only reason I noticed a dark splash on the snow just around the corner from the fire.

It was one of those things that jump out at you because they don't fit. We'd had a fresh snowfall that morning, and everything was hidden under its soft white covering. The dark patch didn't belong, and for that reason I went over to see what it was.

I couldn't quite make it out, because of the way it was lying in a crumpled little heap, so I leaned down and picked it up.

"A mitten," I said out loud, feeling foolish at the discovery. "It's just a mitten." For a second I'd felt like a detective finding an important piece of evidence, only to realize it was nothing at all. I was going to toss it back on the snow so its owner might find it again. My mom used to get annoyed when I was little because I was always losing mitts and gloves.

Then I noticed an unmistakable smell and lifted it to my nose, just to be sure. Yes, it was gasoline! I knew

I should turn right around and take it to the police, and it was probably stupid not to. But by then I'd realized something else about it.

It was probably the upset of the evening, first Nick not coming back and then the fire in the Lawfords' garage, that had kept me from making the connection right away. Something about the mitt had seemed familiar, but it hadn't registered immediately.

It had the same strange design as the pair of mittens Greg Taylor had been wearing when we'd been building the snow sculpture at my place at Christmas. This one was different colors, navy with gold and green, but the pattern was identical.

I'm not sure how long I stood there before I could finally make my legs move again. So many thoughts ran through my mind that my head was starting to spin.

"*My dad knitted them.*"

Greg's words echoed in my brain. I felt like crying. Mr. Taylor was such a nice man, and yet there, a short distance away from the latest scene of a fire, was a mitten that he had made.

It was still in my hand when I got home, and I knew there was no way I could take it into the house without Mom finding it. She has a nose on her like you wouldn't believe, and she'd have noticed the smell and sniffed it out inside of ten minutes. I had to hide it somewhere else.

The storage shed out back would have been a good place, but Dad hadn't shovelled it out today. If I took it there my footprints would only make him ask what I'd been doing out in the shed. Hiding a piece of evidence in a crime was bad enough, I didn't want to have to start lying to my parents too.

Finally, I shoved it under the back step, thinking I'd find a better place for it later on. Or maybe I'd end up taking it to the police and telling them that I'd found it near the fire. It would be hard to explain why I hadn't turned it in right away, but I didn't want to think about that right then.

It was way past eleven by then, and I was hoping the folks would be asleep. No such luck. Dad flung open the door before I even had a chance to touch the knob. His face was worried and relieved all at the same time.

"Shelby! At last! Where on earth have you been, child?"

"I was at Nick's place, helping him with an essay. I told you after supper, remember?"

"Yes. But your mother called there around ten and Mrs. Jarvis told her you'd left. I drove over to their house and back, but there was no sign of you. And now your mother has gone out on foot looking for you."

"Uh, there was a fire a few streets away. I went over to see what was going on. I didn't realize how late it was."

He frowned, but I could tell he'd already heard something about the fire. Or maybe he'd heard the sirens. Either way, he knew I was telling the truth.

"That's still not a very good excuse, dear. You know better than to be out this time of night without letting anyone know where you are."

"Sorry." I just wanted the conversation to be over with so I could go to my room and get to work on the science project. It wasn't that easy though. Mom had come back in and, after hugging me, she kept me there for a good ten minutes giving me one of those lectures that says the same thing over and over in about four hundred different ways. To be honest, I hardly heard a word she said. When people lecture me I usually find that I've tuned them out after the first minute or so. Not that I'm rude or anything, it just seems a waste of energy to keep on listening after the point is made.

When she was done I apologized again and hurried up to my room. I heard Mom close their bedroom door a few minutes later, but I waited for nearly half an hour before turning my light back on and booting up my computer to get information for my project. Mom would hit the roof if she knew I had spent the evening helping Nick when my own schoolwork wasn't even done.

It was nearly two in the morning when I finished the project, and I have to admit it wasn't what you'd call impressive. The best I could hope for was a passing mark, which meant I was going to have to work really hard for the rest of the semester if I wanted a decent grade in science.

As tired as I was, it was hard to get to sleep. And when I did, I dreamed that Nick was laughing at me while I knitted mittens.

CHAPTER TWELVE

I was really tired the next morning, which almost caused an argument between Betts and me. Of course, she was wound up over the new excitement of another fire, and she took my yawns personally.

"Do you have to do that?"

"What?"

"Make it so obvious that you're not interested in what I'm saying."

"Honest, Betts, it's not like that at all." I told her how I'd been up late working on my project, without going into anything about what had happened earlier in the evening. If she knew I'd been to Nick's place, she'd want all the details. I wasn't about to admit to her or anyone else that I'd written an essay for him while he was out all evening. I couldn't tell her I'd been at the fire either, because she'd interrogate me mercilessly.

As far as the mitten went, I had no intention of telling anyone about that. At least not yet. Maybe somewhere deep inside I was hoping that Mr. Taylor was still innocent, and I didn't want to be the one who caused him trouble for nothing. It was hard to convince myself he wasn't involved when a mitten he'd knitted was near the scene — and had gasoline on it. The best I could do was to try not to think too much about it right then.

She seemed to accept my explanation that the reason I was yawning was just because I'd been up so late and continued talking about the fire.

"This is so creepy," she whispered, as if the culprit could be right behind us listening in. "My parents were saying that they're going to get a security system with a really loud alarm. Who knows where the next fire will be?"

"Maybe it's just a coincidence that the Lawfords' garage caught on fire. I mean, they haven't finished investigating yet. It could have been caused by something other than someone setting it on purpose."

"Yeah, right. And it just happened that the fire started when no one was there. Like all the others." Betts sounded more than skeptical at my theory. To be honest, I didn't think it was a real possibility myself.

"All I'm saying is that it could be that way."

The bell rang before we could discuss it any more, and I have to admit I spent a pretty miserable morning in class. Being tired made it hard enough to concentrate on what the teachers said; with everything else in my head, it was just about impossible.

Lunch finally came, and I was glad for the break from trying to pay attention to math and history. Betts met me at the lunchroom, and we picked up where we'd left off. Then I saw Nick walking toward us, and I wanted to crawl away somewhere. It was only a matter of seconds before he'd get to the table and say something that would tell Betts I'd been at his place. She'd be furious when she found out I'd kept it from her. I jumped up quickly, saying that I'd be right back, and headed toward the girls' bathroom.

Nick caught up with me on the way.

"Shelby!"

I turned and faced him squarely without saying a word. I guess he could see I wasn't too happy.

"I'm so sorry about last night. I feel like such a jerk."

"Yeah?" I wasn't letting him off that easily.

"I swear I thought I'd be home right after practice, but something came up. I can't explain it right now," he reached out and touched my hand, "but please trust me. I didn't mean to leave you there alone all night."

I felt my anger dissolving with his hand on mine and his eyes all sad and full of regret. He really did look sorry.

"It's okay. I just didn't know what happened."

"I wish I could tell you, but I can't. A friend needed my help for something personal."

"Forget it."

He smiled then, and I found my knees going to rubber as I smiled back.

"The essay was awesome by the way. Thanks a lot."

"You're welcome."

"I guess you heard about the fire last night."

"Everyone has."

"Yeah." He paused like he was about to say something else, but he didn't.

"Well, I have to go." I hoped he'd tell me to wait, maybe suggest that we do something together on the weekend to make up for last night. Instead he just gave my hand a quick squeeze, said thanks again, and wandered off.

I spent a couple of minutes in the bathroom so Betts wouldn't get suspicious, then I went back to our table.

"What did he want?" she asked before I even had a chance to sit down again.

"Who?"

"Nick! I saw you talking to him in the hall."

"Oh, nothing much. Just something about the fire. Everyone's talking about it."

"Did he see anything?" she asked.

"Like what?"

"You know, the fire."

"Why would he have?"

"I just thought, since he was out last night, he might have noticed something."

"How do you know he was out?"

"I saw him. My uncle was over at our house, and I can't stand him, so I went out."

"Oh, yeah? Where'd you go?"

"Nowhere really, just around. Oh, there's Graham. I have to ask him something. See you later."

She flew off then, leaving me to finish my lunch alone.

I could hardly wait for the afternoon classes to end so that I could go home and get some rest. Then I saw the e-mail notification on my computer screen, and when I checked there was a message from an unfamiliar sender.

"Meet me at The Scream Machine at 6:30 P.M.." There was no name given, but the sender's e-mail address was CoolJ@LittleRiver.ca. I looked around for my school newsletter, which had a page for students to list their e-mail addresses, but couldn't find it.

It had to be Nick, I thought. Who else could it be? The J must be for Jarvis. I smiled then, remembering how he'd looked as though he wanted to say something else when we were talking. Maybe he was nervous because of last night and couldn't bring himself to ask me out when we were face to face.

Instead of taking a nap as I'd planned, I rushed through my homework, promising myself that I'd put more effort into my schoolwork from now on. Then I told Mom where I was going and headed out.

I was a few minutes early. Nick hadn't arrived yet, so I slid into a booth to wait. To my dismay, in walked Greg.

"Hi Shelby," he paused by my table. "Anyone sitting here?"

"I'm waiting for someone," I said shortly. He wasn't going to ruin things for me this time!

"I'm working tonight," he said, not taking the hint. "I have a half hour break for supper so I thought I'd grab a bite here."

"You'd better hurry then."

"It's been pretty quiet at work this week," he went on. "Last night I spent most of my time cleaning because there were hardly any customers. It was so slow that Mr. Broderick closed at nine instead of ten."

"People don't go out as much in the winter." I willed him away with all my might while watching the door for Nick.

"I guess not. Well, my burger should be ready. I called it in a few minutes ago. See you later."

"Yeah, see you."

The door was opening then, and I thought I was going to scream. Of all the bad luck, Jane Goodfellow stood in the doorway. It was almost comical, like everyone in town was working against me. She looked around and then walked over to my table.

I wondered what I could say to her. It would be so awkward when Nick got there.

She stopped and took a seat directly across from me. There was something different about her, and it only took me a few seconds to realize that it was her hair. She'd worn it long and parted in the middle ever since I could remember, but now there were bangs over her forehead. They were way too short, and I thought the new style made her look silly. *She* probably thought it was chic though.

"Thanks for coming." She smiled thinly. "I didn't know if you'd happen to check your e-mail in time to get my message."

She had sent the e-mail? I hardly had time to adjust to this bit of news before she dropped another bomb on me.

"Anyway, I heard that you did Nick's essay for him yesterday."

"Who told you I did Nick's essay?" I asked, startled.

"He did. I saw him last night when he was on his way home from practice, and we talked for a bit."

So *Jane* was the friend who needed him for something personal! I was so angry I could hardly speak, considering that some of the time I'd been working on his essay he'd been with Jane. I could picture him with her, not caring that I was alone in his kitchen while she probably flirted with him shamelessly.

"You aren't doing him any favours, you know."

"I really don't see what business it is of yours, Jane." I knew I'd spoken more harshly than was necessary and that it was really his fault that I was so upset.

"It's my business because I care about him. He has to learn to do his own work or he'll never get anywhere."

"But he'll get cut from the team."

"So let him. That'll be his problem, not yours. He knows what he needs to do to stay on the team." She paused and looked hard at me. "You probably think I'm jealous or something, but it's not about that. I wouldn't go back out with Nick if he asked me to."

I just bet you wouldn't, I thought. I was just about to say something that may not have been very nice when Greg caught my attention, waving as he headed out the door on his way back to work at Broderick's Gas Bar. My eye was drawn to something blue sticking out of the pocket of his jacket.

It was the other mitten, the mate to the one I'd found near yesterday's fire!

CHAPTER THIRTEEN

You can just imagine the thoughts that were racing through my head by the time I got back home that night. The fact that Jane was being a busybody and interfering in my upcoming romance with Nick would normally have had me steaming, but after seeing the mitten in Greg's pocket it was the last thing on my mind.

A few different theories presented themselves to me, and I suddenly realized that this was exactly what the whole town did. They got an idea and ran with it and expanded it until it grew into an actual story. In my case, though, I was just trying to figure things out, not spread random gossip under the pretence of it being based on fact.

Well, there were a few possibilities all right, and only one of them could be true. I studied the whole thing from different slants, until my head started to hurt from the effort.

The most likely theory, of course, seemed to be that Greg was the Little River fire starter. Why else would the mate to the mitten I'd found near last night's fire be in his pocket?

He'd already admitted that he was off work early, and that gave him plenty of time to set the fire and still be home at the usual time. The more I thought about it, the more positive I was that I'd solved the crime.

The question was, what was I going to do about it? I knew I should go to the police, but something held me back. Maybe it was the way I'd treated Greg at times, or it might have been the fact that I felt sorry for him because his mother was dead. In any case, I decided to wait for just a little while before doing anything.

I figured that if Greg was indeed the one setting the fires, the chance that he'd strike again in the next week or two was low. After all, there had been none at all for months. Maybe this one would even be the last.

Then I got to wondering what made a person do something like that. I guess it would be easy enough to understand how a kid in Greg's position might flip out and do weird things after his mom had died in a fire.

A really chilling thought occurred to me then. What if he had set the fire that had killed his mother? As impossible as it seemed, I had to face the fact that a few days earlier I'd have laughed at the idea that anyone as mild mannered as Greg Taylor might be involved in the local fires.

Even if I was wrong about Greg, at least one thing was pretty clear. One of the Taylors was the culprit. The mitten I'd seen couldn't belong to anyone else, since it was handmade in that unusual pattern.

As much as the evidence pointed to Greg, I didn't rule out his father completely. He could have been wearing his son's coat the night before, but there was no way for me to find that out.

Or was there?

It suddenly hit me that I was in an ideal position to find out things that no one else could, partly because of the evidence I had, but mostly because if I was careful I could do it without arousing suspicion.

If the police started nosing around asking questions, Greg and his dad would certainly clam up. But if I started hanging out with Greg, it would be normal for me to stop by his place now and then. That would give me opportunities to look for clues and ask innocent sounding questions.

It was at that moment that I decided for sure I was going to keep what I knew to myself. Once I had more proof I would go to the police.

I might as well admit that the thought of being a hero of sorts had its appeal. I'd go from being just another student at the school to being someone everyone talked to and wanted to be around. I'd never had that kind of popularity before. I thought I could stand it.

Of course, there was a downside to the whole thing, and that was how I'd keep working on getting Nick to ask me out if I was spending time with Greg. It would certainly complicate things, but there had to be a way to convince Nick that Greg and I were just friends. And as Greg himself had pointed out, it might even pique Nick's interest.

I started planning my next move.

It was pretty exciting, but I also knew it might be dangerous. I thought I should have some kind of insurance in case I ever found myself in a tight spot. That was when I decided to start writing all this down.

I envisioned a scene where Greg had knocked me unconscious and dragged me into an empty building. He would splash gasoline around, all the while feeling this awful anguish over having to kill me, the only girl he had ever really wanted. Just as he lit the match, my eyes would flutter open and I'd say weakly, "I wouldn't do that if I were you."

"Oh, yeah? And why not?" he'd ask, because that's the way it always happens. Killers can never resist talking to their victims; I'd seen enough movies to know that much.

"Because if you do, you'll be going to jail for murder instead of just facing arson charges. Guaranteed."

"They'll never catch me!" he'd insist, his eyes half mad.

"They won't have to. I already did, and once I'm dead everyone will know it."

"How?" he wouldn't sound so sure of himself then. He'd blow out the match, waiting for my answer.

"Because I have it all recorded and hidden away in a place where it will be found if anything ever happens to me." I'd smile to show him just how unafraid I really was.

"I don't believe you." His voice would be shaky though, and I'd know he was wavering.

"Well, believe it or don't believe it, it's still true. It's all there, every last detail, starting with the mitten I found near the fire at the Lawfords'."

"Mitten?" he'd gasp, remembering that he'd lost one that night. Sweat would break out on his forehead, and his face would be pale and frightened.

"Yeah, it's hidden too, and my notes will lead the police right to it. I'm afraid you're heading for prison for a long, long time, if you kill me." As he looked more and more worried, I'd continue.

"On the other hand, if you let me go, things will probably go pretty easy for you. After all, you're young and you lost your mom in a fire. The court will probably be understanding and just give you probation or something."

Then he'd put his face in his hands and tell me how sorry he was and that he never wanted to hurt me. Of course, I'd be kind and understanding.

Afterward we'd go to the police, and he'd confess to the fires and tell the police how I'd solved the crime single-handedly.

The newspapers would do some front page stories about me then. Heck, I might even be on the six o'clock news. But through it all I'd be modest and just insist that I had only done my civic duty, or whatever it is that heroes say at times like that when they want everyone to know how humble they really are.

After that much excitement, even if it was only in my imagination, it was kind of hard to get to sleep.

CHAPTER FOURTEEN

By the end of the next week, things were coming together better than I could have imagined. First of all, Nick had asked me to go to a movie with him on Friday night. That was on Wednesday, but on Thursday he had to cancel because his aunt was coming to visit, and his mom said the family should stay home to make her feel welcome.

I was a little disappointed, but I didn't let it bother me too much. After all, it proved he was interested, and he was sure to ask me again before long.

At the same time, I'd been talking real friendly to Greg, making it clear that any hard feelings I'd had in the past were over with. He warmed up quickly, and we chatted a few times at school. Since Nick was going to be stuck in the house on Friday, I figured it would be a good time to start my investigation in earnest.

I casually asked Greg if he was working that evening, and when he said no, I told him I was going to The Scream Machine for a while if he wanted to get together for a soda.

"Just as friends," I added quickly to make sure he didn't misunderstand. He said sure, and at seven-thirty that night we met there.

The first thing I noticed when he came in was that he was wearing the jacket he usually wore to school, not the one he'd had on the evening he'd come in to the soda shop when I was waiting for Nick. Well, Jane actually, but I'd thought I was waiting for Nick.

"Is that the same coat you had on last week when you were in here?" I asked casually, as if I'd just noticed that it was different.

"No, that was my work jacket. I only wear it when I'm at Broderick's."

"Do you ever wear this one to work?" I asked, nodding at the one he had on.

"Naw, this one's new. I don't want to ruin it."

It was pretty exciting to have the answer to one of my questions that easy. Now I knew that Greg had been wearing the jacket that held the mitten I'd seen on the night of the Lawfords' fire. That pretty much eliminated any chance that his father was the one who'd set the fire, since they couldn't both have been wearing it.

Then I realized that didn't prove that the mittens were in that jacket that night. Still, it was a piece of the puzzle. I was sure that once I'd gathered all the facts I'd have the whole picture.

"Something wrong?"

I started when he asked that, and realized that I'd been lost in thought and not paying any attention to what he was saying. It wouldn't do to make him suspicious.

"Oh, sorry," I laughed nervously and took a sip of my root beer. "I get daydreaming sometimes."

"Don't apologize," he smiled and leaned forward. "I do it all the time. The worst is when I'm in school and I realize I haven't heard a word that the teacher has said the whole class."

That kind of freaked me out. I thought I was the only one who got lost in my own head that way. It felt strange to know that this pyromaniac did the same thing.

Well, I wasn't about to let something like that distract me from my plan. I plunged forward with the next part, trying to look as though something had just occurred to me.

"Darn! I meant to ask you to bring me a couple of books."

"What, tonight?"

"Yeah, I have nothing to read right now," I sighed heavily, wondering if he was buying it.

"I could bring you some tomorrow," he offered.

"That would be okay, I guess." It wasn't the answer I'd been hoping for, so I didn't even have to pretend to be disappointed.

"Did you really want something for tonight?"

"Well, no. It would be a bother for you to have to go all the way home and back." I perked up as if I'd just had a sudden thought. "Unless ...," I hesitated, then said, "never mind."

"No, tell me what you were thinking." He was making it so easy!

"We could walk out to your place and get some, I mean, if you don't mind or anything."

"That's a great idea! Then you could have a look and pick out whatever you want to borrow."

"That would be awesome, if you're sure you don't mind."

Of course he insisted then, and we set off toward his house. It was about twenty minutes away, but the night was nice: cold, but clean and fresh. The walk actually took away some of the fatigue I'd felt from having so much happen and not getting enough sleep lately.

Halfway there I had an inspiration.

"My hands are freezing," I said, rubbing them together and blowing on them. "I wish I'd thought to bring my gloves."

"I think I have some mittens with me," he said

right away, digging in his pockets to check. "Yup. Here they are."

It was the same pair he'd had on when we were building the snow sculpture at Christmas. I reached for them, but he was holding one open and slipped them onto my hands one at a time.

"Thanks," I said, feeling almost guilty that he was being so nice when I was just trying to get evidence on him.

"Hey, these are the mitts that caused the argument with you and Betts," I laughed as if I was just remembering it. "It was kind of a silly thing to fight about."

"I didn't fight with Betts," he said, looking genuinely surprised. "Not agreeing with someone isn't the same thing as fighting."

"Sounded like a fight to me," I said, then realized I was getting off track. Before he could answer I added, "But I guess you're right, it was really just a difference of opinion."

He took a sideways glance at me to see if I was being sarcastic but must have been satisfied that I meant it because he said no more on the subject. We chatted as we walked and I tried to focus on what was being said even though I was trying to think of another way to bring up the mittens without it looking deliberate.

When we got to his house and I peeled them off I got my chance.

"Thanks, they were really warm. It's neat that your dad made them, too. Does he knit very much?"

"Not a whole lot. He says it's relaxing, kind of takes his mind off things when pressure builds." Greg smiled a bit sheepishly. "I tried it a few times but I couldn't really get the knack."

"Well, I think it's nice that he made you these." I paused, wondering if I was pushing it too far. "Has he made you other things?"

"A few." Greg leaned to unlace his boots and hauled them off. "Well, let's have a look at those books."

Disappointed that I hadn't been able to get him to mention the blue mittens, I followed him into a room where bookcases had been erected against every wall. It was amazing, like having a library right there in the house. I noticed that there were photo albums on the bottom of one shelf, and beside them a small pile of scrapbooks. If only I could have some time alone in the room I could look through them to see if there were any news clippings from the fire that killed Mrs. Taylor.

"This is my section," Greg said, waving toward one full wall of books. "Just have a look and help yourself to anything you want."

He sank into one of the three oversized chairs in the room as I stood peering at row after row of titles. After a moment, Mr. Taylor came along.

"Why hello, Shelby." He smiled and nodded. "I thought I heard voices in here."

"Hi, Mr. Taylor. Greg is lending me some books."

"Excellent," he perched on the arm of a chair. "It's a chilly night out there, would you young people like something warm to drink?"

"Oh, Shelby, you have to try my dad's hot chocolate!" Greg stood. "It's the best."

I said that would be great, pushing down feelings of guilt that they were being so nice. What would they think of me when they found out the real reason I was there?

Mr. Taylor disappeared into the kitchen, and after I'd picked out a couple of books we joined him there. He set three big steaming mugs on the table. They smelled heavenly.

I took a sip and couldn't help exclaiming that it was indeed the best hot chocolate I'd ever tasted. There was a plate of cookies too, and they were delicious as well. As I was eating my second cookie I commented on the interesting flavour, something that came through the dates and cinnamon with a slight nutty taste.

"Flax seed," Greg's dad told me. "I like to make up my own recipes, like these cookies, and put in healthy things like flax."

"You're awfully talented," I smiled at Mr. Taylor. "Why, Greg tells me that you even knit. I wore the mittens you made on the way here and they were lovely and warm. Interesting pattern too."

He beamed at the compliment. "I've made four pairs in that pattern, two each for Greg and me. They tend to be warmer than what you buy in the stores."

"Actually, I only have one pair now, Dad," Greg commented as he bit into a cookie. "I lost a mitt from the blue pair the other night."

My heart did a little flip-flop then. Now I knew for sure that it was Greg who had been wearing the mitten I found near the Lawfords' fire.

Chapter Fifteen

In spite of everything that was going on, I was asleep almost as soon as my head landed on the pillow that night. The next thing I knew, Mom was nudging me and telling me to get up.

"Whaaa?" I couldn't quite get the whole word out.

"You're wanted on the phone." She smiled and ran her hand over my forehead. "Do you want me to tell him to call later?"

I squinted at my alarm clock and saw that it was after eleven o'clock in the morning. Mumbling that I was awake, I slid out of bed and headed groggily for the kitchen.

"Hello?" Did you ever notice that when you answer the phone, it always sounds more like a question than a greeting? It's almost as if you're not necessarily going to be happy to find out who's on the other end of the line.

"Good morning." It was Greg. "Am I waking you?"

"Yeah, but it's okay. I didn't mean to sleep so late."

"Well, sorry about that. Anyway, what are you doing later?"

I hesitated, wondering if Nick might reschedule our date at the theatre for that evening. He hadn't said how long his aunt was going to be staying, but it was probably more than just one night. There was no sense losing a chance to dig up more clues.

"Nothing much. Why?"

"I'm at work right now, but I get off at two o'clock this afternoon. I thought you might like to hang out later on."

The thought of the scrapbooks on the shelf at his place flashed into my head. I sure wanted to get a look at them.

"Well, you'll have to go home to change after work, right?"

"Yeah, that won't take long though."

"Why don't I meet you there around three? We can decide if we want to go anywhere else then."

"Sounds great." His voice was really happy. "I'll see you then."

After I hung up the phone I showered, dressed, and had a bagel with strawberry cream cheese. While I ate I tried to think of some way I could get a look at the scrapbooks.

A knock at the door interrupted my thoughts, and when I looked up I saw Betts standing there. The expression on her face told me something was wrong.

I'd no sooner let her in than she burst into tears.

"Graham and I are through!" she wailed, throwing her arms around me. "He's nothing but a big jerk and I hate him."

Her remark seemed kind of at odds with the tears. After all, if she really hated him, there'd be no reason to be crying over their breakup.

"What happened?" I asked, patting her shoulder with my free hand. The other hand still held a piece of bagel, and the way her shoulders were heaving I was sure she was going to get cream cheese on herself. I held it as far from her as I could as I led her to the table and got her into a chair.

"He said I'm suffocating him," she sniffed loudly, "and he needs his space."

"Well, in that case, you're right. He's definitely a jerk. You're better off without him."

"But I like him so much!" she howled, contradicting what she'd said less than a minute ago. "How could he do this to me?"

"Guys are weird, Betts, you know that. Sometimes they break up with girls because they like them too much and they can't handle it."

"You think he broke up with me because he likes

me a lot?" The idea seemed to interest her, and it looked for a few seconds as if she might stop crying.

I nodded emphatically. "I bet that's it all right. He probably got scared by his own emotions. Mom told me how that can happen. Something about commitment phobia."

"Commitment phobia," Betts repeated slowly. She sniffed again. "But what do I do about it? If he's scared to like me, he's never going to go out with me again."

"Not necessarily." I tried to remember the details of some of the talks Mom and I had had about relationships. "I think that if you handle it right, he'll end up being more interested in you in the long run."

"How?"

"Uh, let me see. Don't call him, don't go out of your way to talk to him, pretend you couldn't care less. And never let him see that you're sad or upset."

She looked doubtful, but at least she wasn't crying anymore. "I'll try it," she said, lifting her chin. Then she added, "You're lucky, you know."

"How come?"

"'Cause your mom talks to you about stuff like this. My mother hardly ever has time to talk about anything. She's always too busy."

I felt good about that. After Betts left I went to look for Mom to tell her I was going to Greg's for a while. I thought I might like to give her a hug too.

I checked through the house and found her just coming out of her darkroom. I told her about my plans for the day, and then noticed that she had just hung some new pictures up. They looked pretty good.

"Can I see these?" I asked, pointing to the wall where clips held them in place.

"Sure. I was getting some nature shots the other day, but I don't think I quite captured what I wanted to."

I stepped into the room and peered at the glossy black and white pictures. There was one of a squirrel sitting on a branch, its eyes bright and alert.

"This one's really good," I commented as my eyes travelled along the others. My gaze stopped suddenly as I spied a picture of myself walking away from the school.

"Hey! That's me."

"Goodness, how did that happen? I must have mistaken you for a raccoon or something."

"Mom!" Her jokes were pretty dumb sometimes, but I'd usually laugh anyway because of the way she'd giggle when she told one.

"I have quite a few pictures of you that you didn't know were being taken. I like them a lot because they're so natural."

"Can I see the rest of them?" I was surprised and naturally curious.

"They're here, in this folder." She hauled open a filing cabinet drawer and pulled out one of the pale yellow folders nestled inside, passing it to me. "Be sure to put them all back when you're through."

Then she headed toward the stairs, calling over her shoulder, "I'm off to Ethel's place now. I told her I'd be there by two o'clock, but it never hurts to be early."

Ethel is a neighbor of ours who has multiple sclerosis. Mom helps her with her housework once a week, just out of kindness. That's what my mom is like.

I opened the folder and was about to start looking through it when something in what she'd just said jogged in my brain.

It never hurts to be early.

What if I showed up at Greg's place at two instead of three? I could pretend I'd gotten the times mixed up and then just ask his dad if I could look at more of the books while I waited for him. It was perfect.

I stuck the file back into place and hurried to my room to get ready. If I walked quickly, I could be there well before Greg got home.

It was five minutes after two when I reached their house. I figured that still gave me enough time to at least get a quick look at the scrapbooks, since it would take Greg twenty minutes to walk home from Broderick's. But when I knocked on the door, there was no answer. I went around the back of the house, just in case Mr. Taylor was outside, but there was no sign of him.

That was when I noticed a thin curl of smoke coming from the far side of their storage shed.

I ran around the shed to get a better look and saw that flames were just starting to lick the outside of the building. I scooped snow on it frantically to smother the flames before they got out of hand. They sizzled and sputtered for a few moments and then went out.

Looking around, I noticed that the snow had been stirred up and there were pine needles laying in it here and there. I followed the trail it created out to the street where a broken bough lay discarded. Whoever had been there had taken care to cover their tracks.

I was still standing there when I saw Greg coming along the street. He raised his arm in a wave and called my name cheerily.

As he got closer, I blurted out what I'd just discovered and we went together to examine the damage to the building. It was minimal, a few scorched areas where the flames had begun to burn before I'd put the fire out.

"Thank goodness you were here," Greg said solemnly. "That building is pretty close to the house, and there's a breeze blowing this way. It wouldn't have taken much for the house to catch too."

"It would be awful to lose your house for the second time," I commented.

He looked hard at me then, and I blushed when I realized what I'd just said. He'd never mentioned anything about the fire that had claimed his mother's life, so it had to be obvious to him that I'd been listening to the town gossip.

"Yes, for the second time." His eyes bored into me and for a second I felt afraid, although I wasn't really sure why. It felt as though he was looking for something that I didn't want him to find.

CHAPTER SIXTEEN

We went into the house then, and Greg called the police to report the fire. While we waited for them to arrive I mulled over some perplexing questions. The big one, of course, was who had set the Taylor's shed on fire? It couldn't have been Greg, since he was nowhere near when it happened. And where was Mr. Taylor? Was it possible that he knew Greg was responsible for the other fires? He might have heard the rumours that centred on him and figured that if the police were watching him, they'd soon realize that the culprit was actually Greg. Could have set his own building on fire in order to draw suspicion away from his son?

The police cruiser pulled into the driveway before I'd had a chance to work my way through this new tangle of clues. Greg got up to meet them at the door. He explained that I'd been the one who'd discovered smoke coming from the shed, and they asked me a bunch of questions and then got me to sign a written statement.

I felt a little guilty when they asked me if there was anything else I could tell them. I knew they meant about the fire at the Taylors', but it didn't make me feel any better when I said there was nothing else, since I had a key piece of evidence under the step at my house. That reminded me that I'd meant to move the mitten to another hiding place, but I couldn't worry about that right then.

They were there for almost an hour, and Mr. Taylor still hadn't come home. Greg was surprised that his dad wasn't there and hadn't left a note or anything.

"He always leaves a message telling me where he'll be if he's going out," Greg commented to me after the police left. "It's strange that he didn't this time."

Strange unless he expected the house to be on fire by the time Greg got home, I thought. In that case, leaving a note would be a waste of time. Naturally, I kept that thought to myself.

"Well, I've got to get cleaned up and changed," Greg said then. "I won't be long."

"No rush," I assured him, meaning it. "Do you mind if I have another look at your library while you're in the shower?"

"Of course not. Make yourself at home."

I listened carefully as he headed upstairs and was pleased to hear several squeaks when his feet touched some of the old wooden steps. Reminding myself to stay alert so that I'd hear the same sounds when he was returning, I grabbed a book from one of the shelves and sat on the floor beside the spot that held the scrapbooks. All I'd have to do was put them back when I heard him coming and pretend to be looking through the book.

Still, my heart was pounding as I reached for the first volume of family mementos. It held a collection of cards, many of them handmade by Greg, the kind you do in school for special occasions for your parents. I flipped through it quickly and stuck it back in place, taking out another.

In the pages of the second book were pressed flowers and leaves, tiny bags of sand, and similar tokens from nature. Among these were snapshots of Greg's parents, sometimes both of them, sometimes just one or the other. Greg appeared in a few too, and each page was neatly labelled in fine script with details of the date, place, and occasion. It was like a trip through day-to-day events that had been part of the family's life: a day at the beach, a walk through the woods, and vacations they had taken.

I fared no better in the third book, finding more pictures, ticket stubs from movies or social events, napkins from restaurants, and other such souvenirs. There were now only two scrapbooks left to look through. I glanced nervously toward the stairs, listening. To my relief I heard water running, which meant Greg must still be in the shower.

A surge of excitement ran through me when I opened the next book and found that it contained newspaper clippings. The first few were their engagement and wedding announcements, then there were some that must have been about friends or relatives of the Taylors. There was a clipping about Mr. Taylor's appointment at the university, and a few about organizations in which they were involved. I turned the pages impatiently.

"Blaze Claims Life of Local Woman." At last! Something about the fire! I scanned through the columns, reading the story as quickly as I could. It was a pretty factual account, telling only that the fire had broken out during the night, that father and son had escaped but that Mrs. Taylor had not. It ended with a statement that the cause of the fire was under investigation.

I turned the page and the next heading leapt out at me: "Arson Suspected in Fire at Professor's Home." The beginning of that story basically recounted some of the details in the first story, but then it went on to say that investigators believed the origin of the fire to be suspicious.

"We're not ruling anything out at this point," the fire marshal was quoted as saying, "but evidence points toward the fire having been deliberately set."

I drew in a deep breath, finished the rest of the story, and then looked across to the next page. The heading there read simply "Culprit Found!" As my eyes shifted to the first line in the body of the story I was stunned to see that it began with the words "Greg Taylor".

"May I ask what you're doing, Shelby?"

The scrapbook went flying out of my hands, and I jumped to my feet and whirled around to find Mr. Taylor standing in the doorway. I'd been so intent on listening for Greg's approach that I hadn't even thought of his father. Now he stood there, his face a cold mask of politeness. In spite of that, I could see anger in his eyes.

"I was just waiting for Greg," I stammered, feeling heat rush to my face.

He didn't answer. Instead, his eyes moved to the scrapbook, now lying open on the floor. I started to bend down to get it, but he lifted a hand up, like a little stop sign, and moved towards it himself.

Culprit Found. Greg Taylor... The words pounded in my head even as I tried to think of some reasonable explanation for what I'd just been discovered doing. I watched as Mr. Taylor reached for the scrapbook and looked to see what I'd been reading. He folded it closed and sat it carefully back on the shelf with the others. As he straightened up to face me again, Greg bounded down the stairs and into the room.

"Hey, you're home." Speaking to his father, Greg's smile faded. He could see that something was wrong and naturally assumed it was about the fire on their property. "I guess Shelby filled you in on what happened."

"Shelby," his father told him with the calm tone of a person holding anger in check, "was otherwise occupied when I arrived."

"Then you don't know about the fire. When Shelby got here the shed out back was just starting to burn. She put it out with snow." Greg smiled proudly in my direction as he finished speaking.

"Our shed? Our shed was on fire?" Mr. Taylor sounded dismayed but there was no real shock in his voice.

Greg gave his father the detailed account of the fire. I glanced at Mr. Taylor's face a few times but was still too mortified to look at him for long. It was hard to tell, from quick peeks, whether he was truly startled by the news or just acting a part.

"Where were you anyway?" Greg thought to ask his dad. "There was no note or anything when I got home."

"As a matter of fact, I was called into town suddenly. Actually, I was sent on a wild goose chase."

"What do you mean?"

"I received a phone call from a young lady who told me you'd been hurt at work and were being taken to the hospital." He paused, considering. "Obviously it was a ploy to get me out of the house. Now that I think about it more, she may have been trying to disguise her voice."

Mr. Taylor turned then and stared at me. Surely he didn't think I had made the call! It looked very much as if he did.

"Why would anyone do that?" Greg asked, missing the look his father had given me.

"Perhaps the caller wanted to make sure I was gone so she could set the fire. Or perhaps she had something else in mind, and the fire was a coincidence. Why don't you ask your friend here what she was doing when I came into the room?"

"What *were* you doing, Shelby?"

I couldn't find my voice to answer him, so his father did.

"The truth is, son, this *friend* of yours was snooping through our family scrapbooks."

Greg looked shocked, and I couldn't help but wonder, even in my embarrassment, if it was because he was afraid of what I'd seen.

Culprit Found. Greg Taylor...

"Now, Miss Belgarden, I'm afraid I'm going to have to ask you to come with me."

"What are you going to do to me?" My voice was barely a whisper.

"I think you already know that, Shelby. You've really left me with no choice."

As soon as he said that, I knew Mr. Taylor had figured out that I knew Greg was the one setting fires. He was going to have to silence me to protect his son.

The scene I'd imagined only days before came rushing back at me, only it didn't seem so exciting any more. My stomach twisted in knots and a cold shudder ran through me.

There was only one thing I could do. I lifted my chin and tried to keep my voice from shaking.

"Wait! I know that you want to protect Greg, but I have it all written down. And I have evidence that proves it. If anything happens to me, you'll both be arrested."

CHAPTER SEVENTEEN

A stunned silence greeted my announcement, which gave me a little more courage. I swallowed hard and braced myself to make a run for it if either of them came any closer to me.

"What evidence are you talking about?" Mr. Taylor finally asked. He looked perplexed. I guess he hadn't figured on me having any actual proof.

"The missing mitten," I said triumphantly. "I found it."

"And this, uh, mitten, proves something, does it?"

"Well, of course it does. It proves that Greg is the one who's been setting all the fires around here."

"*I've been setting fires?*" Greg sounded truly astonished, but I wasn't about to let that fool me. "That's ridiculous."

"Is it? Well then, explain why your mitten was

beside the Lawfords' garage when it burned down."

"I don't know. I don't even know who the Lawfords are! I lost the mitt when I was walking around after work one night."

"Oh, really? Then explain why it was covered in gasoline!"

Greg stared at me as though I had suddenly grown an extra head.

"Well, I guess it would have *gas* on it because I work at a *gas* station, pumping *gas*."

It did sound reasonable, but I wasn't in the least persuaded. There were too many things pointing to his guilt, not the least of which was Mr. Taylor's threat only moments before.

"If you're so innocent then, why was your father just about to take me somewhere and kill me?"

"Kill you?" Mr. Taylor sputtered. "Kill you? Heavens to Murgatroid! Where would you get such an idea?"

"Well, you said ...," my voice trailed off and I stood helplessly as they looked at each other incredulously. Then I realized that he hadn't actually said he was going to kill me. I tried to remember his exact words, but everything was getting jumbled.

"All I *said* was that you were to come with me. I felt that I had no choice but to take you home after I found you trespassing so rudely on our privacy."

I could hardly get my thoughts straight. Then I remembered the newspaper article.

"What about the clipping in the scrapbook, the one that says 'Culprit Found'?"

"What about it?"

"I only saw the beginning, but it started off saying 'Greg Taylor'."

Mr. Taylor shook his head, and then he did a most unexpected thing. He began to laugh, and once he got started it seemed he wasn't going to be able to stop. His shoulders shook and tears started down his face.

When he'd calmed himself, Mr. Taylor took the scrapbook out and opened it to the article I'd mentioned. He pointed to the first sentence, and I finally got to read the rest of it.

"Greg Taylor was overcome by tears today as he spoke to news cameras after police announced the arrest of the man responsible for his mother's death."

If ever I look back on my life and need to identify the moment that I felt like a total idiot, that will be it.

"Oh," I said in a very small voice.

"You actually thought I was setting fires?" I could sense Greg's eyes on me as he spoke, although mine remained glued to the floor. "That I would do such a thing after my own mother died in a fire?"

"It seemed that, you know, the mitten and ...," my voice trailed off as I began feeling more and more foolish. Now my accusation sounded so incredibly flimsy that I could hardly believe I'd been so certain he was guilty.

"But *why* would I do such a thing? Did you ever ask yourself *that* while you were playing detective?"

I didn't even attempt to answer that one. To offer any of the theories I'd had would only serve to add to the humiliation I'd already brought on myself.

"And that's why you were looking at our scrapbooks?" Mr. Taylor asked. "Because you thought Greg was involved in the fires in Little River?"

"Yes." I looked at the floor. "I'm really sorry."

"What you did was wrong, Shelby," he said softly, "but at least I can understand your motivation now. I'd thought you were just being nosy. Greg and I have lost a great deal in the last year, but at least we had our privacy. Those books contain things that mean more to us than you can ever imagine. My late wife put most of them together, and their contents were never intended to be pawed through for the sake of curiosity."

He cleared his throat and continued, "However, now that I know *why* you were looking at them, I can see that you must have felt justified, regardless of how mistaken you were."

I think that if he'd yelled at me and thrown me out with the admonition to never come back, it would have been easier. Instead, there he was being all understanding and kind about the whole thing. It made me feel a hundred times worse.

"I think I'd better go," I finally said in what was barely more than a whisper.

"Now, hold on," Mr. Taylor motioned me toward a seat in the room, "let's all just sit down and get this thing worked out. There's no need for hard feelings. And let's not forget that you probably saved our house when you put out the fire in the shed."

I just wanted to leave. At that moment I wanted it more than anything in the world. But I wasn't about to add to my rudeness by refusing, so I sat down.

"You know, Shelby, in spite of the way this all turned out, you can be proud of yourself for examining things and trying to put them together. After all, that's how crimes are solved."

I was feeling anything but proud.

"In fact," he continued, "I don't think you were entirely on the wrong track in one aspect of your deductions."

"What do you mean?"

"I think it's very probable indeed that the person responsible for the fires is a student, either at the high school or junior high level."

"Really? Why?"

"As I told the police when they consulted with me ..." he paused, seeing the surprise on my face. "Yes, that's right. Everyone knows the police came to see me last fall when the fires started. They surmised, incorrectly, that it was because I was a suspect. The truth was that they were looking for my help. Since I am a doctor of psychology, the police felt I might be able to steer them in the right direction with some sort of offender profile.

"Anyway, as I was saying, I told the police they were most likely looking for a younger person. It is very rare for someone to start setting fires later in life. Since Little River has never had this problem in the past, either the culprit is new to the area and has a history of fire-setting somewhere else, or he or she is between the ages of ten and eighteen."

"But how do you know that?"

"Because this particular crime is most often committed by someone who has been victimized as a young child."

"You mean that whoever is setting the fires has been abused?"

"Yes."

"And that's why they're doing it?"

"Sadly enough, that's exactly why, although it's doubtful that he or she realizes it. It's always important to look for a motive or cause for this kind of behaviour."

He stood then and walked over to one of the bookcases. Drawing out a book, he turned back to me.

"Since you're so interested, it might be a good idea

for you to educate yourself on the subject. Unless, per-haps, you've had enough of the whole thing."

The book he held was called *When Children Set Fires*. I reached for it.

"I'd like to read it," I said humbly, "but I think I'll leave the detective work to the police from now on."

"That might be a good idea," he smiled, "but it's also possible that reading this will trigger something that could be helpful to the police. In a small place like this, you must know most of the teenagers at your school. Maybe someone will stand out in your mind as fitting the characteristics in this book."

"Yeah, considering that you have such a fine ana-lytical mind and never jump to stupid conclusions," Greg snapped.

His sarcasm was not lost on me, and I realized that was the first thing he'd said since we'd sat down. His earlier silence made it clear that he was still angry, and I couldn't blame him. After all, I'd just accused him of something pretty horrible.

"Greg, that's no way to speak to a guest in our home."

"I deserved it," I said quickly, half afraid that Mr. Taylor was going to suggest Greg apologize for the remark. "Anyway, thank you for the book and for being so understanding. I'm really, really sorry about every-thing, especially for looking at your stuff."

I stood and said that I really had to go.

"I'd be glad to give you a drive home, Shelby, unless you're afraid I may decide to kill you on the way." His eyes twinkled, and I knew he only meant to lighten the mood.

I blushed at the joke and thanked him for the offer but said the walk would probably do me good.

To his credit, Greg got to his feet and said that he'd walk me home if I wanted. My mom would have described that kind of gesture as a sign of good breeding, being gentlemanly in spite of everything that had happened.

All I wanted, though, was to get away from him as quickly as possible. I mumbled something about needing some time alone and headed for the door.

On the walk home the only thing I could think about was how hard it was going to be to face Greg Taylor at school on Monday.

Or ever again, for that matter.

CHAPTER EIGHTEEN

I felt so miserable by the time I got home that all I wanted to do was go to my room and stay there. Walking quietly, I hoped my mom wouldn't spot me and see that something was wrong. But it was my dad who intercepted me in the hallway.

"Finally, another human being!" he smiled and hugged me. "I thought I might have been abandoned for the rest of the weekend. Do you know where your mother is?"

"She went to Ethel's place, but she should have been back by now. Maybe she had some shopping to do or something."

"Maybe. She wasn't expecting me home until after dinner, but here I am. And hungry as a bear at that. How about the two of us go over to that spot where you kids hang out and get something to eat?"

"The Scream Machine?"

"That's the place. Unless it wouldn't be cool to be seen there with your old man."

There was no point telling him that old man meant boyfriend now. My dad is great, but he's hopelessly locked in what I call The Parental Time Warp.

The last thing I felt like doing was eating, but since we hardly ever get time to do anything, just the two of us, I really couldn't let him down.

"It would be way cool," I assured him.

"Is that bad?"

I laughed in spite of my misery. "No, it's good."

"Way cool," he repeated, smiling. "I'll have to remember that. You know a cat like me likes to be hip to your jive."

"Dad! Promise you'll just talk normal when we're there!"

"Don't worry, I'll act my age." He stooped over. "Just let me get my walker."

I rolled my eyes and laughed at his teasing. I knew he'd never embarrass me in front of my friends.

We left a note for Mom and then headed out. The Scream Machine was nearly empty when we got there, and we snatched a booth quick before it started to fill up. Since it was nearly five o'clock, the crowds would be landing soon. There are always a lot of kids there at meal times on the weekend, but I didn't mind being there with my dad. Besides, I figured that once word got around of what a fool I'd made of myself at Greg's place, I would be spending a lot of time at home with my parents. At least I could count on Betts to stick by me. Good old reliable Betts.

Dad ordered a Scream Burger Special, which has three meat patties, cheese, bacon, and fries on the side. I ordered the soup of the day without even asking what kind it was.

"It might be best not to tell your mother about this," he whispered, with the tone of a conspirator, when his food arrived. Mom has been known to run interference when he's trying to get certain things out of the fridge, lecturing him on cholesterol all the while.

"My silence can be bought," I whispered back.

We were laughing and talking and having a pretty good time when I was jolted by the sight of Nick coming in with Kelsey Princeton. He'd danced with her a few times when Jane didn't show up for the Christmas formal, but I didn't think he was actually interested in her. After all, he'd been acting interested in me! I felt the smile freeze on my face and tried to pretend I didn't notice them, but Kelsey made sure I did.

"Hi, Shelby," she cooed in a sickeningly sweet voice, stopping at our booth. Nick stood behind her and didn't look at me.

"Uh, hi, Kelsey, hi, Nick." I did my best to offer a smile as phony as the one she'd given.

"And this must be your date," she giggled in a high-pitched squeak.

"Actually, Kelsey, this is my father." I spoke slowly, as if I was explaining something to a small child. Then I made quick introductions while hoping that they choked on whatever food they ordered.

"What a nice couple," my dad commented a moment after they'd moved on. "Are they friends of yours?"

"They're just some kids from school." I couldn't help but be thankful that it was Dad with me and not Mom. She'd have seen through the smiles and seemingly polite talk and would have asked me questions that I wasn't in the mood to answer. Dad, on the other hand, was pretty much oblivious to everything except his burger.

After seeing Nick with Kelsey, I felt even more wretched than I had earlier. Dad went to the counter to ask for more coffee, and I could hear her giggling on and on and on. I could only hope the sound was getting on Nick's nerves as much as it was mine.

Then something happened that I could hardly believe. Annie Berkley came in to pick up a take-out order. I could see Nick and Kelsey giggling quietly to each other as they watched her pay for her food and head back towards the exit. As Annie swung the door open, Kelsey made a loud oinking sound.

Everyone froze. Well, almost everyone. Nick and Kelsey both laughed while Annie's face got red, and I could see that she was biting her bottom lip as she hurried outside.

Then my dad spoke up, his voice carrying through the silence in the room. "Well, well, I guess there are pigs in here all right," he said calmly. "Yes indeed. A couple of them right over there at that table."

And just like that the attention swung around, shifting to where my dad was pointing, straight at Nick and Kelsey. They stopped laughing and looked down at their food. Then someone started to clap, and before I knew it, everyone was clapping and saying things like "Yeah!" and "That's right!"

When Dad came back to our booth I told him I was really proud of him.

"I wish I had the courage to do something like that," I added.

"Ah, I just did what everyone else wanted to do. No one likes that kind of deliberate cruelty. When a thing like that happens, it's important to remember that the way you feel about it is most likely the way others feel too."

"Well, I know one thing, Dad. You're way cool."

Nick and Kelsey left pretty fast after that, and I tried to tell myself I didn't care if he was with her or not. I suddenly understood how Betts was feeling about

Graham, hating him and liking him all at once. It's not something you can always control, the way you feel about a guy. As slimy as he'd just acted, I found myself making excuses for him.

For the first time ever, I really wished I didn't like Nick Jarvis.

Well, it wasn't going to matter much anyway. I'd be the last girl he'd ever ask out once word got around of what I'd done that afternoon.

It seemed at that moment that my life was pretty much ruined for the rest of my high school years. I'd never be able to live it down once Greg told everyone about my stupid accusation.

It was like the time Bobbie Jean Rayford told everyone she'd won a trip to meet some rock star, and we found out later that she'd made the whole thing up. That was years ago, but it still came up from time to time. She'd been something of an outcast ever since, keeping to herself and trying to ignore the fact that no one really wanted to hang around her. She had a label that she couldn't get rid of, and I knew I was about to have one too.

It was hard to believe that a week that had started out so great could end so horribly.

CHAPTER NINETEEN

I spent most of the next day keeping myself busy so I wouldn't be dwelling on thoughts of how my life was about to change for the worse. I started reading the book Mr. Taylor had lent me, and before long I was so immersed in it that I almost forgot about my problems.

There was a lot of stuff about safety issues and how a large number of fires were started accidentally because of kids fooling around with matches or lighters. I skipped those sections because it was pretty obvious the fires in Little River were no accident.

Other chapters explained things about certain childhood disorders and how playing with fire was sometimes connected to them. They seemed to be talking about much younger children. It was kind of interesting, but not what I was looking for.

The book was hard to understand in some places,

and I had to keep looking words up in the dictionary. It seems that psychologists have a language of their own. That made reading it pretty slow, but it wasn't like I had a lot of other things to do.

The most interesting parts of the book were where the author gave examples from actual cases, although the names had been changed. It was kind of scary to read how some of them had even set fires in their own houses or at their schools.

Mr. Taylor had talked about kids setting fires because they'd been abused, and before long I got to that part of the book. I was shocked to find out that the kind of abuse he was talking about was sexual abuse. I'd expected it to be about kids who had been beaten or starved or locked in a closet or something.

When we were in elementary school we learned about good touches and bad touches and stuff, but none of the things in this book were discussed then. Our teacher had gone through it all pretty fast and had seemed to be embarrassed talking about it. Still, we all knew from watching different TV shows that sometimes adults hurt kids in that way. But this was Little River, and I always figured that kind of thing didn't happen here.

Then I got to a place where the author was talking about statistics! I could hardly believe my eyes when I read that one out of every four girls and nearly as high a percentage of boys were victims of sexual abuse. It made my head hurt to even think about it.

I sure didn't know anyone who had ever been abused like that. Why, I hardly knew of anyone who had been physically abused either. Then I remembered that Annie had been taken away from her folks when she was eleven and had been living in different foster homes ever since. I wondered if anyone had ever hurt Annie that way.

One out of four girls! I tried to think of all the girls I knew and started writing their names down. There were almost fifty names by the time I finished my list, though a lot of them were kids I didn't really know all that well. Fifty girls. If the statistics were right, it was a safe assumption that about twelve of them had been sexually abused! It seemed impossible.

Well, it was a girl who had called Mr. Taylor and told the story that sent him to the hospital just before the fire was started at his place. That seemed to prove that the culprit in Little River was female.

Or did it? What if it was a guy and he'd had a girl make the call? Or what if he'd disguised his voice? Considering the alarming nature of the phone call, Mr. Taylor might have been fooled quite easily.

The statistics suggested a boy was just as likely to be guilty as a girl. Sighing, I took out a fresh sheet of paper and made another list, this time writing down all the boys I could think of. By the time I'd finished I had over a hundred names altogether. The task seemed more daunting than ever.

One thing had become very clear to me as I'd worked my way through Mr. Taylor's book: the question of *who* was setting fires in Little River had suddenly become far less important than *why* he or she was doing it.

If someone was burning places for the sake of destruction, you know, out of meanness, it would have been one thing. But from what I had read, this person was doing it for different reasons altogether. The fire starter was hurting inside, and hurting bad.

There are about four hundred students at Little River High, and I had only been able to think of a quarter of them. I was just thinking that the whole thing was hopeless when the phone rang. It was Betts.

"Shelby, get your skates and meet me at my place!"

I laughed at the familiar way she launched into a conversation without saying hello or anything first. When Betts is excited, she doesn't waste time on small talk.

"What's up?" I asked.

"We're all going to the Green Pond. They cleared the ice this morning and it's perfect. Hurry!"

The Green Pond sits near some residential properties on the edge of town and has been a popular place for skating ever since I can remember. The water is so still that it freezes as smooth as any rink. A few years back the town set up dusk-to-dawn lights there so that we could use it in the evenings. This would be the first skating party there this year, and I rarely miss one. I decided to go, hoping that no one had thought to invite Greg. It was the last chance I had to hang out with friends before he spread the news about my accusation.

When Betts and I got there about half an hour later I was relieved to see that Greg was not among the gathered crowd. The air was crisp and clear, the way it usually is after a recent snowfall, and the stars looked like distant snowflakes sparkling in the sky. The whole scene was lovely, and I almost wished I was there alone. All the shouts and laughter detracted from the still beauty of the place. But it was more than that.

After all my reading and list-making earlier in the day, I found it impossible to look at the skaters without thinking about the statistics I'd just learned. As friends flew past me, whizzing along the ice, I couldn't help looking at their faces and wondering.

One in four girls and close to the same percentage of boys. How many of these seemingly happy skaters carried dark secrets? I found myself picturing those around me crouched beside a building setting a fire. Some of the mental images almost made me laugh, they were so ridiculous.

But others were not nearly so funny. I found it strange how easy it was to picture some of the kids with lighters in hand, their faces intense. It was scary.

There was Laurie, a girl in the eleventh grade, gliding along the ice in her sad, quiet way. Or Meredith, with her boyish clothes and typical tough act. Jane's pouting face and angry eyes flew past, while Annie circled slowly with her vacant smile. It seemed to be hiding pain a lot of the time. And Kelsey. What might be hidden behind her defiant and haughty face?

For some reason I found it harder to imagine the boys as victims, even though statistics proved they were just as likely to have been abused. Like the ultra macho Nick, skating alone as he usually did because none of the girls could keep up with him. Then there was Todd, at Annie's side most of the evening, until he joined Nick in building a bonfire at the pond's edge. Though this was something we always did, the sight of the flames sent shivers through me.

Graham was nowhere to be seen, and it was obvious that Betts was disappointed he hadn't made an appearance. I shuddered, suddenly remembering him at the dance mimicking a girl's voice.

When we gathered around the bonfire to roast the marshmallows several of the kids had brought, I felt almost sick to my stomach. The flames danced, reflected in the eyes of those circling the fire. I couldn't help but think that one of the group gathered there might have watched other fires burn. What would go through a person's mind at such a time?

By the end of the evening, I found that I'd been able to picture over a dozen of the kids who were present in the role of fire setter without any problem at all.

Now, I knew that just because I could envision someone doing it, it didn't mean they were really capable of burning down buildings. And I knew, after yesterday's fiasco, that my instincts weren't always great.

But I was getting more and more interested in the whole thing, and something inside me didn't want to let it go. Besides, maybe if I figured out who was responsible, I could redeem myself from the embarrassing incident with Greg.

There was a chapter in the book that talked about common indicators of sexual abuse. When I got home I wrote them down so that I could consider each of them with the students on my list later on. It would take too long right now, and I was getting tired from thinking so much.

I stuck a marker in place and closed the book. Before I got into bed, I looked at the names on my lists again and pictured the faces of each person written there.

One of them might be the guilty person all right, but I didn't want to figure out who it was in order to see him or her exposed and punished. Whoever was responsible for the fires needed help!

CHAPTER TWENTY

"Don't you think Derek Browning is yummy?"

"Derek? I guess he's all right. Why?"

"Why? What do you mean, why?" Betts' face was indignant as she looked at me from across the lunch table. "Do I have to have a reason for every little thing I say?"

"No, but you usually *do* have a reason, and when it's about some guy or other, it's usually because you like him." Seeing her smile I added, "C'mon Betts, out with it."

"Well, he is pretty deelish, I have to admit." Betts likes to say deelish instead of delicious.

"What happened to your plan to get Graham back?" As I spoke I saw Greg walk into the cafeteria and seat himself with a bunch of kids from his class. I braced myself for the hoots of laughter and stares that would be coming once he told them about what I'd done.

"Graham is after Jane now." A hint of something bordering on anger flashed across her face and then was gone. "And she can have him for all I care."

"How do you know he's after Jane?"

"Because he's all over her, there on the other side of the room."

I looked in the direction she'd nodded at, and sure enough Graham was sitting with his chair pulled up as close as he could get it, laughing and talking to Jane.

"That doesn't mean she's interested in him," I pointed out.

"Well, she might as well be. I'd say that the two of them are perfectly suited to each other, seeing as how they're both snobs. Why, would you believe that Jane came to school this morning with a new winter jacket? She just got one at Christmas and now she has another one."

"Maybe there was a sale."

"No, wait, I'm not finished telling you this! I heard Holly saying how she loves Jane's new coat this morning at the lockers. So Jane tells her thanks, she hated the one she got at Christmas, and Holly says, but Jane, you picked that out yourself, I thought you loved it. And Jane says she hates it now."

"Breathe, Betts!" I laughed.

"Stop interrupting. You won't *believe* the next part. Then Holly asks Jane if she can have the other coat, the one she got at Christmas, since Jane hates it anyway. And what do you think Jane says to her?"

"I'd have to guess that she either said yes or no."

"Nope. She says, sorry, she threw it out. A practically brand new jacket, and she threw it out. Now that's snobbery! Which, as I said earlier, makes her perfect for Graham."

"Yeah, well it's pretty obvious that Jane wants Nick back, so Graham is probably wasting his time."

"Well, good luck to her then, because Nick likes someone else now."

"Kelsey?"

"No, not her. What would make you say that? She chases him all over the place, but he's not interested."

"It's odd that they were together at The Scream Machine on Saturday then."

"She probably cornered him and dragged him in. I know for a fact he likes someone else."

"Whatever." I didn't want to hear who it was, even though I was trying hard not to care about Nick.

"Whatever? I'd have thought you'd be more interested, seeing as how you used to have a big crush on Nick."

"That was a long time ago," I lied.

"Too bad then, because it's you."

"What's me?"

"It's you that Nick likes, what do you think?" Betts looked exasperated at my failure to grasp her meaning right away. I suppose my slow uptake had sort of robbed her of the reaction she'd hoped for in making the announcement.

I'd been waiting nervously for the onslaught of jeers and snickers that I knew would soon be headed in my direction. So far there'd been nothing, but the story was bound to spread fast once it hit. Betts' statement broke through those thoughts and sent a different kind of shiver through me from the one I'd been waiting for.

"Where did you ever get such a silly idea?" I finally asked.

"From Nick himself."

I did my best to look as though I wasn't overly interested in what she was saying, but couldn't help asking, "Why, what did he say to you?"

"He said that he thought you deserved a chance."

"That I *deserved* a chance? What's that supposed to mean?"

"You know, like he's thinking about giving you a shot as his girlfriend."

"Did he say that too? That he's going to *give me a shot*?"

"Yeah. You don't look very excited," she frowned. "What's the matter with you anyway? Nick is *such* a stud!"

"Well, the things he said to you are not exactly flattering, Betts."

"Why not?"

"Because it sounds like he's, you know, granting me a big favour or something. Like he's stooping to give me this huge opportunity to be *his* girlfriend."

"I thought you'd be pleased. I know you're not gone on him like you used to be, but he's still a pretty big catch around here."

"I'd kind of like to go out with someone who thought *I* was a big catch too, Betts."

"Then you might as well give in and go out with Greg Taylor. You know he's mad for you. I mean, if you're looking for someone to idolize you like that, he's the one. Nick doesn't have to go crawling to girls that way. He can have anyone he wants."

"Well, he can't have me," I was surprised to find myself saying. I might have a change of heart later, but at the moment I meant it, and it made me feel proud. "So he might as well not waste his time asking."

"Get out of here! You would *seriously* turn down Nick Jarvis?" Betts giggled at the thought. "Boy, I'd like to be watching when that happened. I don't think anyone has ever said no to him."

"He probably won't even ask me out," I said, thinking of how he'd react to the news of my detective work. It was strange that no one was talking and pointing yet.

Greg must be stretching the story out, building it up to the big finish. Or maybe he was biding his time, making me sweat.

"Oh, I think he's going to ask you all right," Betts sounded positive. "From what he said to me, he's planning to make his move pretty soon."

I thought of Annie's face, the hurt and embarrassment on it when Nick and Kelsey were laughing at her on Saturday. It was one of the meanest things I'd ever witnessed. Suddenly I hoped with all my heart that he *would* ask me out just so that I could turn him down flat. For Annie.

Then I thought of how he'd sucked me into doing his essay and how stupid I'd been to spend the whole evening alone at his house doing his schoolwork. Other things came to mind, things I'd dismissed because he was such a package. When I looked honestly at what I knew about him, I had to admit that Nick was not exactly a nice person. He was conceited and arrogant and very careless with other people's feelings.

So, just like that, I let it go. All the years of dreaming of the day that he'd ask me out dissolved in that moment. Now that it seemed it was actually about to happen, I knew with absolute certainty that I would never go out with Nick Jarvis.

CHAPTER TWENTY-ONE

Lunch hour ended and the afternoon classes passed without me hearing a single snide remark about my inept sleuthing. I caught glimpses of Greg a few times, but he never once looked in my direction. It was almost as if he was aware of my presence and determined not to take any notice of me.

By the final bell, I was pretty much a basket case. It's like when you're young, and you know you've done something wrong, and you're waiting for your parents to find out. I remember once I knocked over my mom's jewellery box, and the mirror inside the lid came off and broke into little bits all over the floor. I gathered them up and hid them in the kitchen garbage, but I knew that the next time she opened that box I was busted.

The thing was, I didn't know how *often* she got jewellery out. Mom isn't the fancy type, and she mostly uses that kind of stuff for special occasions. So I was waiting and waiting to be found out. It seemed like months passed, and sometimes I'd forget all about it, but then I'd be in her room and see it sitting there on top of her dresser and I'd be reminded. Every time, I got this sick feeling in my stomach, until it finally got to the point that I just wished she'd find out what I'd done and get it over with.

When she finally noticed it, there was this huge relief. I was sitting on her bed and we were talking while she folded laundry. She looked at her watch a few times and then got this questioning look on her face and took it off.

"Hmmm. The battery must be dead," she said, laying it on her night table. Well, Mom is one of those people who always says she feels lost without a watch on, so it was no surprise that she went to get the one she wears when she goes out somewhere. She opened the jewellery box, and I could see that she was puzzled. She stared at it for a few seconds before it clicked in that something was missing.

"That's odd," she said. "I wonder what happened to the mirror."

Of course, I burst into tears and sobbed and sobbed. Mom stared at me, first in astonishment and then in alarm.

"Why, Shelby, honey, it's all right." She wrapped me in her arms and held me while I bawled out how sorry I was and that I hadn't meant to do it.

"I know you didn't, sweetheart. But why didn't you just tell me when it happened?"

And that was the thing that stayed with me, how I'd suffered for all that time when all I had to do was go and own up in the first place. I should have known that Mom wouldn't be upset over something like that.

Well, this was different, but the feeling was the same, that horrible waiting to be found out. Only this time there was no chance that anyone was going to tell me it was all right. I wondered how long Greg was going to take to spill the whole story.

By Wednesday I was an absolute wreck! Every time I heard someone laugh I was sure that it was starting. Betts noticed that something was bothering me and asked a few times where my head was at and what on earth was wrong with me. Part of me wanted to tell her the truth and get it over with, but I just couldn't bring myself to do it.

I should be able to trust Betts, seeing as she's my best friend and all. But it's hard when she's so interested in every single thing that's going on around her, especially things that have gossip value. For example, right from the time the fires first started, she clipped every single newspaper story on the subject, and had even started a scrapbook just for that. It was kind of amusing in a way, since she normally acts as if reading is worse than a trip to the dentist. In any case, I said nothing to her. It would have been a hundred times worse if she spread the story about my stupidity than if it came from Greg.

Then, after school on Wednesday, my worries were interrupted by another small drama. As with any other day, there were quite a few kids standing around, some of them waiting for their buses and others just chatting before heading home. I'd been trying to find a notebook in my locker, so I was a few minutes late coming out of the school. That was when Nick called out to me.

"Shelby. Over here."

"What do you want?" I called back. It seemed rude of him to summon me that way, instead of just coming over.

"I want to talk to you." He was wearing that smile that could always make me weak in the knees, but this time it wasn't affecting me at all.

"Then *you* come *here*," I said.

I thought that might make him mad, since he's not used to being refused. But he just smiled again and sauntered over.

"I've been thinking," he stretched his words out, like he was creating some big drama, "that the two of us would make a pretty fine couple."

He sounded very sure of himself, and that just annoyed me more. I said nothing.

"So, what do you think, babe?" He was standing in what I couldn't help think was a posed stance, with a finger tucked into the belt loops on his jeans and his chest thrust out.

"What do I think about what?"

"About what I just asked you." His smile was fading fast, and I could see impatience on his face. I guess he'd expected me to swoon and gush that it would be wonderful, or something like that.

"You didn't ask me anything," I pointed out. "You just made a comment."

People were looking and listening. I could feel it, and I knew he could too. He had to turn things around fast or he was going to lose face.

"You want the big question do you?" he forced another smile. "Well, I guess I can do that. So, what do you say about us hooking up?"

"Thanks, Nick," I answered evenly. My heart was pounding and I didn't know why. "But no thanks."

"No?" He looked incredulous. "You have to be kidding."

"Why would I be kidding? It was nice of you to ask, and I appreciate it, but you're really not my type." And then I walked away.

I could hear the buzz of voices behind me, and I have to admit it felt pretty good to know that Nick Jarvis, the great jock, had been turned down right in public and that I was the one who had done it.

Maybe now he'd have some small inkling of how Annie had felt when he and Kelsey had embarrassed her so cruelly. I guess that was stretching it though. Nick wasn't the type to give much thought to anyone else's feelings. He might be humiliated, but he'd never make the connection with how he'd made someone else feel.

Betts called me the second I got in the door at home.

"You actually did it!" she almost screamed. "You said no to him. I can't believe it."

"I didn't know you were even there when it happened," I laughed, remembering what she'd said yesterday and pleased that she'd gotten her wish.

"I was talking to Derek," she explained. "He is *so* dreamy! Anyway, we heard the whole thing. Everyone there did. You should have seen Nick's face when you walked away. He was furious!"

"I'm sure he'll get over it," I said dryly, "the only person Nick is really into is himself. He couldn't date someone who doesn't feel the same way about him that he does."

That made Betts giggle, but it also reminded me of how Greg had once told me that Nick was totally wrong for me. I wondered if he'd been around when I'd refused Nick.

I found myself hoping he had been, although I had no idea why it mattered.

After all, even if I was interested in Greg, which, I hastily reminded myself, I was *not*, there was no way we would ever end up together now.

CHAPTER TWENTY-TWO

When I'd finished talking to Betts, I saw that there was a note on the table. It was from Dad, explaining that he and Mom had gone over to Veander, a nearby city, and would be late getting home. I peeked in the fridge, knowing that Mom would have left a plate for my dinner. Sure enough, there was cold chicken and pasta salad waiting for me.

I closed the fridge, not yet hungry, and began wandering through the house in boredom, trying to think of something to do. Then I remembered the pictures I'd been about to look at on Saturday. You know, the pictures I'd set aside so that I could go make a big fool of myself at Greg's place.

I brought the file upstairs from the darkroom and spread it out on the kitchen table where the light was good.

There were quite a few, and it was fun looking through them. I was surprised to find one of Betts and Greg and me in the middle of our snow fight on Christmas Day. In that shot, Greg was standing behind me to the left, his hand poised with a snowball that he was clearly about to lob at Betts. She was crouched down, laughing, her hands scrunching snow into a ball. I seemed to be yelling something while I brushed a clump of snow off my jacket.

I closed my eyes and tried to recapture the moment in memory. When I looked again, I noticed that even though Greg was aiming at Betts, his eyes were directed at me. There was a smile playing on his mouth, and I could almost read his thoughts. If I was right, he was definitely thinking something nice — about me.

Well, I'd sure put an end to that!

I flipped through more pictures and found that a number had been taken last year at a big picnic the school had organized one Saturday in June.

I noticed Jane standing next to Nick in one shot from the picnic. She'd been after him even then. It was weird that when he'd finally asked her out she never wanted to go anywhere with him. She wasn't in any of the other pictures taken that day, and I recalled that she'd left early, looking resentful as usual, when her step-father came by for her.

There were a couple of shots of us around a fire we'd made for cooking hot dogs. Peering closely at the expressions on the faces around the fire, I was struck by the fact that a few of the kids looked almost hypnotized by the flames. I giggled at the sight of Annie, who seemed to be in some sort of deep trance.

It's neat the way looking through pictures brings back memories, things that you'd never think of again otherwise. It made me realize just how many details we have stored in our brains. You think that little things are gone and that you'll never find them again, but they're actually just tucked away, waiting in case you ever need them.

By the time I'd finished looking at the pictures, eaten, and done my homework, I was ready for bed. I was almost asleep when I heard a tap on my bedroom door, and Mom and Dad came in to say goodnight. That was the last thing I remembered that day!

Thursday and Friday passed quickly, and there were definite reactions to the fact that I'd turned Nick down. Some girls were outright admiring and made comments to me about how glad they were that I'd put him in his place. Others were scornful and made no secret of the fact that they thought I was insane for passing up such a hot guy.

None of that mattered much. I knew I'd done the right thing for me. There were a few moments of regret, but they disappeared fast when I reminded myself that he really wasn't such a great person after all. I think maybe his popularity was partly responsible for him being the way he was: if you've gone through school riding on popularity and looks, there's not all that much incentive to also be nice. Nick had always gotten what he wanted because of the way he looked and his status on the sports teams. When you think about it, those aren't really very good reasons to admire a person, but they'd worked for him. When it came right down to it, I figure he'd learned to expect certain things because the way everyone treated him had made him feel like it was his due.

It didn't take long to see that I'd made an enemy for life. Nick made more than one comment about me that wasn't what you'd call polite, and he sure didn't worry about keeping his voice down when he did it. The first one I heard caught me off guard, and I was too stunned to react. After all, it wasn't as if I'd done anything horrible to him. Girls turned guys down all the time, and vice versa. Not many of them felt the need to go around hurling insults because of it.

The next time I heard a nasty remark I was prepared. I walked right up to him and said that I was sorry if I'd hurt his feelings. I made sure my voice was as loud as his.

"As if!" he sneered. "You should have known that the only reason I asked you out was because I felt sorry for you."

"The way you're acting now looks more like you feel sorry for yourself," I retorted. "I realize that your pride is hurt, but you don't have to make it so obvious."

"Who do you think you are?" he yelled angrily. "You're *nobody*, that's who. A big, fat, ugly nobody."

"Come on, Nick, let it go. I'm sure there are lots of other girls who'd love to go out with you. And why wouldn't they? After all, you're so *nice*."

Laughter met my final comment and Nick whirled around in fury, glaring at the gathering crowd.

"Give it up, man. You're no match for her."

I was astonished to see that it was Greg who had spoken. Silence descended on the group so fast it was unbelievable. The students were kind of holding their breath, waiting to see what Nick was going to do next. There was no way he could allow a guy to talk to him like that without doing something about it. Sure enough, he turned to face Greg.

"Shut your mouth, pansy boy, or I'll shut it for you."

"Be my guest." Greg smiled evenly. He took a step forward.

"You don't want to mess with me," Nick warned menacingly.

"Sure I do." Greg's smile got wider. "I'd love to." He looked as though he meant what he'd said, although I couldn't picture him in a fight. Nick fought dirty and mean, and no one ever took him on.

And then the most amazing thing happened. Nick backed down! He mumbled that it wasn't worth getting kicked off the team, turned around, and walked away.

As everyone drifted away, whispering to each other about what had just taken place, I glanced at Greg. For a second he met my eye, but then he looked away and walked off. That gave me the strangest feeling, a hurt that started in the pit of my stomach and spread out all through me.

I wished I could just talk to him, even for a few minutes. I wanted to tell him that I was honestly and truly sorry for last Saturday and to thank him for speaking up to Nick like that. The way he was avoiding me at school, there was no way I was going to get a chance to do it, though. And I sure couldn't go to his place. It looked hopeless.

It wasn't until Friday evening, sitting in my room, that a solution popped into my head. What if I went to Broderick's when he was working on Saturday? It was possible he'd tell me to get lost, but I felt that I had to try.

Satisfied with this plan, I picked up the book his dad had lent me. I was almost finished reading it and had filled half a writing tablet with notes on the subject. My lists of names were there too, but I hadn't found the time to compare the signs and symptoms in the book with the names.

I wondered what I would do if I found that some of the kids fit the patterns. That *might* mean they'd been victims of sexual abuse, but it didn't mean that any of them were guilty of setting the fires. I wasn't keen on the idea of jumping to any more wrong conclusions!

I went through my notes carefully and separated the symptoms into two categories. Some of them, like nightmares, were things that you'd only know if you were living with the person. That wouldn't be of much use to me. The other list was the one I would use as a reference and included the things I might be able to figure out.

This is what I had:

- Secrecy — because of shame, guilt, embarrassment, or fear of what the person who had hurt them might do if they told
- Withdrawal from others, loners (they feel this has never happened to anyone else)
- Unable to trust (difficulty forming strong attachments)
- Academic problems (performance below abilities)
- Depression
- Fear or dislike of certain people or places
- May not be willing to change clothes in front of others

The book had stressed that lots of people can have some of these things for other reasons. Lots of girls at school don't like to change in front of anyone in gym class, but that could just be shyness. Most victims showed more than one of the symptoms.

It was clear that even if I identified possible victims, it was by no means going to tell me who the fire setter was.

There had to be other clues, things related to the fires themselves. I had a nagging feeling that there was something right there in front of me, if only I could figure out what it was.

CHAPTER TWENTY-THREE

It had been my intention to go to Broderick's and talk to Greg first thing after breakfast on Saturday. Whether or not he listened to me and accepted my apology, I figured it would be good to get it over with. Somehow, though, every time I thought about going out the door I came up with a reason to wait. I must have been more nervous than I realized, or maybe part of me was scared. After all, I only had one shot at it, and if he put me off there'd be no second chance.

I'd rehearsed what I was going to say to him a few times in my head, but I knew from experience that was usually a waste of time. There had been lots of times in the past that I'd gotten myself all hyped up and ready to say exactly the right thing about something, and then I'd opened my mouth and it had come out all jumbled and dumb.

That's almost as bad as when you think of all the things you could have said after something's already over and done. That happens to me a lot too.

Anyway, by one in the afternoon I had run out of excuses for putting it off, so I tossed on my jacket and headed out. I didn't exactly rush on the walk over, but even so I seemed to get there in no time.

When I first arrived, Greg was inside talking to Mr. Broderick. He's a nice old guy who sometimes lets us have car wash fundraisers for school sports teams on one side of the lot. He'd always joke with us, and I think he really liked kids, although he and his wife never had any of their own.

Anyway, as I said, Greg was inside at first, so I stood off to the side and waited. Before long a car drove in, and he came out and tended to the customer. I almost lost my nerve and turned around to leave, but then he happened to look up and saw me standing there.

Well, it was now or never. I took a deep breath and started walking toward him, wondering if he'd even wait around or just go back inside. He waited.

"Hi," I said when I'd almost reached him.

"Hello," he said stiffly.

"I'd like to talk to you, if you have a minute."

"I suppose." On a scale of one to ten, the enthusiasm in his voice was about zero.

"Look, Greg, I just wanted to tell you how sorry I am about everything. I made some pretty bad mistakes, but I wish you could believe that I didn't mean anything personal in what I did."

"It was a bit personal to find out someone I thought was my friend was only hanging around so she could dig up evidence against me, or whatever it was you were doing."

"I know that, Greg. I do. And I wish it never happened. It was just that I got carried away with the idea, and I didn't stop to think things through well enough."

"Well, just forget it. It doesn't really matter now."

"It does matter. You're a good guy and you didn't deserve to be treated like that." I stood there feeling kind of awkward and not knowing quite what to say next. It was clear that Greg didn't really want to talk to me.

"Well, you said you were sorry." He paused. "I don't suppose that was easy."

"It was hard to come here and face you, but I had to do it." My voice was catching because my throat was all dry and tight. "Anyway, I hope you can forgive me."

"It's not really a question of forgiving you, Shelby. It's more a matter of being clear about where things are between us. And I think I'm pretty clear on that. So let's just say it happened and it's over and that's the end of it." He turned to walk away.

"Wait, there's something else." I felt panic rise in me. For some reason, I just couldn't stand the thought of our conversation ending like that, with things the way they were.

"What?"

"I want to thank you too, for a couple of things. First of all, for not telling everyone at school about it."

"Why would I do that?" He seemed genuinely puzzled.

"Well, to get back at me, I guess."

He shook his head. "You have a remarkably high opinion of me, don't you?"

"I didn't mean ... I just thought ... most people would have talked about it, and, uh...," I gave up on what I was trying to say, but he finished my sentence anyway.

"And embarrassed you," he sighed. "Unlike some people, I'm not in the habit of deliberately hurting my friends."

"Greg, please! I didn't mean to hurt you." I felt tears filling my eyes and blinked hard to hide them. I had this crazy thought that I wanted to throw my arms around him and make him understand how I felt. I guess that was the moment that I actually understood it myself.

Greg Taylor was the nicest guy I'd ever known. He was smart and funny and decent. I burned with shame to think that I'd missed seeing all of those things until it was too late, and all because I had this big crush on a total jerk like Nick.

"Okay, okay," he looked alarmed, and I knew he could see I was fighting tears. "I'm sorry for saying that. It wasn't called for."

"And I wanted to thank you for sticking up for me with Nick." There! I'd said everything I came to say. All I wanted to do now was go home and cry and get it all out of my system.

"You didn't need any help, girl," he smiled, and I could tell he was picturing the scene again. "You were doing just fine on your own."

"Even so, it was really nice of you."

A car pulled in to the pumps just then, and Greg nodded towards it.

"I have to go," he said, but the door of the gas bar opened and Mr. Broderick came out.

"I'll get them," he called to Greg. "You finish talking to your little friend."

"Well, I guess that's all I had to say anyway, except maybe that everyone was amazed that you were ready to take Nick on."

"You mean in a fight?" he asked. When I nodded he laughed, "I didn't think it was going to come to that. At least, I hoped it wasn't. I'm not much for fighting."

"But it sounded as if ..."

"Don't get me wrong, I wasn't going to back down. I just figured he would."

"How did you know?"

"Because guys like Nick are really cowards at heart. It scares them when someone stands up to them. He had to be wondering why I wasn't afraid, and that made him so nervous he couldn't take a chance."

"You were bluffing!"

"Of course I was."

"But what if he'd called your bluff?"

"I'd probably have gotten my butt kicked."

I realized suddenly that we were smiling at each other, and a little lurch of happiness ran through me. Almost at the same time I could see that Greg had become aware of it too. His guard went back up immediately. It was as if a cloud came over his face.

"Anyway, I've got to get back to work."

"Uh, okay then. See you."

He went back inside without once looking back to where I stood, even though I willed him to with all my might. Then I went home, threw myself across my bed, and cried.

Chapter Twenty-Four

Sunday was a lazy kind of day, and I decided it was a good time to do some more work on my investigation. Well, I like to call it an investigation anyway, although it's probably just a waste of effort.

I took out a fresh tablet and wrote down the different symptoms, with a page for each one. I spread them out on my desk, picked up my lists of names, and started through them.

That took a long time, and I soon saw that some of the categories were going to be really hard to fill in. Like depression. How did I know if someone was depressed or not? Everyone has different personalities, and I really didn't know if the kids who might seem depressed were just naturally quiet or moody or whatever.

It got discouraging pretty fast. I was doing my best, but a lot of it was guesswork. I realized that it would take a trained professional to properly diagnose most of these things. They probably have tests they can give people to prove whether or not they're depressed or withdrawn or can't trust others.

Still, there were a few that seemed to fall naturally into place. Like Annie Berkley. She has a suspicious attitude in general, which means she probably isn't very trusting, and she seems really down a lot. She never changes in front of anyone in gym, but that could be because of her weight problem. It probably is. Her grades are good though, so academic problems didn't fit. I didn't know if she had any particular fear or dislike of certain people or places.

Now Jane Goodfellow was easy to figure out for that one! Anyone could see that she *hates* her stepfather. And Jane always goes into a bathroom stall to change even though she has a good figure. I also remembered that she had to go to summer school one year, but mostly her grades are average. I hesitated and then put her name under academic problems anyway, because there are lots of times she gets ragged on for not having her homework done, and it seems as though she's smart enough to get much higher marks than she does. Sometimes she's really tired too, and almost falls asleep in class.

That reminded me of something I'd read in the book, and I picked it back up and flipped through until I found what I was looking for. It was about depression, and how people who are depressed often can't sleep or sleep too much. Being tired in class could mean she wasn't sleeping well. Under the depression category, I added the names of every student I could think of who sometimes seemed really tired in class. Then I put a question mark after them, because I really wasn't sure about it.

Secrecy. That was a tough one too! After all, if someone's keeping a secret, how would you know about it? This wasn't even one of the things you'd tell your best friend. I tried to think of who were best friends with Annie and Jane, but drew a blank. They didn't seem to have any really good friends, although there were a few girls they hung around with at school. That gave me a new idea.

I decided to write the names of anyone who didn't have at least one really close friend under secrecy. After all, if you were secretive it stood to reason that you would keep yourself somewhat distant from others and would be cautious about getting too tight with anyone.

Then I realized that might also suggest you were withdrawn, because people who are withdrawn are generally loners. Anyone without close attachments to other people could be considered loners, at least to some degree.

It surprised me to realize that neither Nick nor Graham had a close friend. They both seem popular but actually don't hang out with anyone in particular. I added their names under academic problems too, because their grades are barely average. I started wondering about the fact that they both tended to date girls for a short time and then dump them. Did that mean they couldn't trust anyone enough to become attached?

As an afterthought, I put a little note beside Graham's name about how good he was at mimicking a female. There are probably lots of guys who can do a girl's voice convincingly though, so that didn't really prove anything.

Then I was jolted by the memory of the evening I'd done Nick's essay. That was the same night the Lawfords' garage had burned! Where had he really been for the two hours after practice, while I'd been working in his kitchen? I knew he'd spoken to Jane, but Nick wasn't the sort to get into long, meaningful conversations. It seemed unlikely he'd been talking to her all that time.

I struggled to recall what he'd said the next day, when he was explaining why he hadn't come back to his house at eight o'clock, as he'd promised. It had been something about a friend needing help, and not being able to tell me the whole story. You couldn't get much more vague than that. It certainly wasn't much of an alibi. Besides, Nick wasn't the type to go out of his way to help anyone. I wondered if my infatuation with him had blinded me to something that was right there in front of my eyes.

Still, there were a lot more names on my lists, and I had learned my lesson about jumping to conclusions. I moved on. As I worked, I thought of some other kids I knew whom I'd missed when I first wrote out the names. I added nearly twenty names, then realized with a start that I hadn't included Betts. That made me smile. Feeling a bit silly, I scribbled her name down, even though the idea that she could be the fire setter was ridiculous. In spite of that, I faithfully went through the information to see if she fit any of the categories.

Betts definitely has academic problems, but then she's just not interested in school. That didn't mean anything. And she never changes in front of anyone, not even me when we're sleeping over at each other's places. Of course that's true of lots of girls. I laughed when I looked at the word "secrecy" seeing as how Betts is such a gossip. She'd be the last person who'd ever keep a secret! It was foolish wasting my time on her when there were so many others in my lists.

When I'd finally finished my task I went through the list of names again, putting a check mark beside each person's name for every time his or her name appeared in one of the categories.

Some of the kids had no check marks at all, and a lot of the others had one or two. But twenty-seven of them had anywhere from three to six out of a possible seven!

It made me feel almost sick to my stomach. I closed my eyes and lay back on the bed, trying to calm the way things were twisting up inside me. These were people I knew, and twenty-seven of them had enough check marks to make me wonder if they'd been abused in that way. Some of them were kids I didn't particularly like because they seemed hateful or standoffish. I'd thought of them as snobs, but now I knew I could be horribly mistaken about that. I'd never be able to look at them again without wondering whether they carried terrible, dark secrets, secrets that affected their lives and made them act the way they did.

My head was aching from concentrating and thinking so hard, and now that I was done I had to admit that I wasn't much closer to figuring out who was setting fires in Little River.

All I had come up with was "maybes." Maybe these kids had been sexually abused. Maybe one of them was the fire starter. Maybe, maybe.

It wasn't enough. I needed something solid, some actual evidence to tie one of them in. The guilty person had to be stopped before someone got hurt.

Most importantly, whoever it was needed help.

CHAPTER TWENTY-FIVE

As the week went by I couldn't shake the feeling that there was something I was missing, something important that would point to the person who was setting fires. By Wednesday, I'd all but given up on trying to figure it out. Short of catching someone in the act, it seemed unlikely that I was going to solve the mystery.

The stir that had been created by the scene with Nick had died down by then, replaced by the fact that he was now going out with Kelsey. She looked like the cat who'd swallowed the canary, as my mom would say, walking around with a look on her face that would have made me glad for her if she hadn't been so mean to Annie.

I reminded myself that Kelsey was one of the girls on my list of possible victims, and tried to feel more kindly toward her. Still, it was hard when she'd been so cruel, and for no reason. Besides, Annie was on the list too.

Greg basically continued to avoid me, and I reconciled myself to the fact that I'd alienated him for all time. I took his books back to him on Monday, even though I hadn't read them yet. It wasn't that they didn't interest me, but it seemed wrong to hang onto them considering that I'd borrowed them under false pretences. (I wonder why people say *false* pretences. It seems that if something is a pretence, it would be understood that it's false.)

Deep down I'd been hoping that we'd have some sort of conversation when I met him at his locker to return the books, but he just took them and thanked me, and that was the end of it. He didn't ask if I'd finished them or anything, just stuck them in his locker and headed off to his next class.

I still had the book his dad had lent me, but I meant to take that to the house sometime when Greg wasn't home. Maybe Mr. Taylor would have some time to talk to me about my method of making up lists. I also wanted to take the blue mitten, which was still stuck under my step, in case Greg hadn't thrown out the other one. It would be embarrassing to have to mention it again, but there was nothing I could do about that.

On Wednesday Betts suggested that she should come over to my place for the evening so we could do each other's nails. She's really talented and can paint tiny scenes on fingernails. I never got onto it very well, but she didn't care if I could only do simple designs on hers.

I told her she might as well come for dinner too, since her folks weren't going to be home. She seemed glad to accept, and I dropped a quarter in the pay phone at school to make sure it was okay with Mom. Of course, it was.

When Betts got there, Mom was in the kitchen mixing up a batch of biscuits to go with the meal. When she found that out, she was keen to go and help. Betts loves to bake, and lots of times when she comes over we'll make cookies or something just because she likes it so much. I guess it's a big deal to her because she and her mom don't do much baking together.

Anyway, we went into the kitchen, and Mom gave her the job of rolling and cutting them.

"Is this too thin?" Betts asked as she ran the rolling pin over the soft dough.

Mom leaned over to inspect and said it was fine.

"Be careful not to get anything on that lovely sweater, dear," she added. I could almost have predicted that she'd say something along those lines. It's kind of comical how Mom is always offering "advice" like that about things that any normal person would know without being told.

But Betts was pleased at being fussed over. "I'll be careful," she smiled, "though this old sweater is second-hand anyway. No, actually it's third-hand."

"Where'd you get it?" I asked. It looked familiar, but I didn't remember ever seeing her wear it before.

"I traded it with Gail for my blue striped top, the one that never fit right."

"So how is it third-hand then?"

"Gail got it from Jane. She gives her all the things she doesn't wear any more because Gail's mom is a single parent and can't afford that much for her. I guess even Jane has a good side. Anyway, the color of this sweater didn't suit her, and I just loved it, so we traded." Betts frowned slightly as she pressed the cutter on the dough. "This seems to be sticking."

"Just dip the cutter in flour between each one," Mom reminded her.

They were ready to go in the oven in no time, and we set the table while they cooked. Dinner was great, roast with potatoes and peas and biscuits. Dad buried everything under gravy, and Betts seemed to think that was a good idea because she did the same with her dinner. There was upside-down peach cake for dessert, with real whipped cream slathered over it, and we all moaned and groaned that we were too full when we'd finished eating.

I volunteered to do the dishes, because I find it helps to get right up and do something when I've eaten too much. Betts came along and dried them, something she never has to do at home since they have a dishwasher.

When we were finished I felt a lot better. Betts had brought along a book of nail designs and her nail polish collection, which is pretty amazing. She has every possible colour you can imagine, so there was nothing in the book that we couldn't do if we wanted to. We spread it all out, along with the brushes she has for doing fine lines, and set about picking out designs.

"Ladybugs for me," she said pointing to a picture in the book. "On yellow backgrounds."

I chose drama masks against red backgrounds, and we started to work on them. Betts's hand was steadier and her lines far more accurate than mine, but the overall results were good for both of us. We showed off the finished products to Mom and Dad, who admired them suitably.

"No one ever offers to do my nails," Dad complained. "Why, I haven't had a good manicure since I don't know when."

Betts grabbed his hand and inspected it carefully. "There's not much hope for you, Mr. Belgarden," she said, shaking her head sadly. "You've just let your cuticles go for too long."

"I've been meaning to do something about those," he sighed heavily while we giggled, "but it's so hard to find time."

I walked Betts halfway home after and then got busy with my homework. I was struggling through some algebra, which I hate, when all of a sudden something popped into my head.

It's funny how your brain works, isn't it? All the time I'd been straining to concentrate and figure things out

I'd been drawing a blank. Then, when I was doing something entirely different, it sorted itself out in my head. I've had that happen before with brain teasers. I'd think and think and be unable to solve them, and then a day or two later I'd be thinking about something else and the answer would pop into my head. It was just like that!

It started with a jolt, a thought that burst into view out of nowhere. Actually, it had been there all along but I hadn't recognized what it meant. Then other things tumbled into the picture and clicked into place. All of a sudden the pieces had all come together, and when I stopped to examine them they all fit perfectly.

I knew who the Little River fire starter was!

CHAPTER TWENTY-SIX

Well, it's one thing to know something and another to prove it. When I wrote down all of the evidence, I had to admit that it was pretty much circumstantial. In a way, it was even flimsier than the case I'd made against Greg, and yet I knew I was right this time.

I wished there was someone I could talk to about it, and as soon as that thought entered my head I realized that the person I most wanted to talk to was Greg. I knew he was the one person who would listen without acting like my idea was crazy or laughing it off. And since he's so smart he might have suggestions that would help me decide what to do about the whole thing. That was certainly the place where I was drawing a blank!

If only I hadn't made such a mess of things between us. Now that I understood my own feelings I wondered why I'd ever thought he wasn't boyfriend material. It was bad enough to accept that I was never going to go out with him, but not being friends seemed somehow even worse.

Still, he'd talked to me at Broderick's last Saturday when he could have just walked away. Maybe there was a small chance I could persuade him to talk to me again.

I couldn't stand the idea of asking him face-to-face and having him refuse me, especially since I'd almost cried in front of him last weekend. Instead, I checked the e-mail list at school, got his address, and sent him a short note. Actually, I composed about ten before I finally had one that didn't seem stupid or pathetic.

"Greg," it said, "I'd like to have your opinion on something important. It shouldn't take long. I'll be at The Scream Machine at 7:00 on Friday evening if you can make it. Shelby."

I sent it on Wednesday. That would give him a couple of days to decide if he wanted to come or not. It also gave me lots of time to worry if it had been dumb to even ask. I was hoping he might send a message back telling me if he was coming, but he didn't.

I'd planned the time to meet carefully, supposing he decided to come. The dinner crowd would have cleared out by then, and anyone who'd dropped in before the early show would be heading off to the theatre down the road. Those going to the late show wouldn't normally start landing at the soda shop until after eight. I'd figured on the place being fairly quiet for an hour, giving me time to explain everything without a lot of other people around.

Ordering a diet cola, I sat down in a corner booth at ten minutes before seven. It was hard not to look at the clock constantly and I wished I'd brought something to read while I waited for him. Every time the door opened I got a flutter in my stomach which turned into a feeling of letdown when it wasn't him. By twenty after seven it wasn't looking good and by seven thirty I swallowed my disappointment and left.

My allowance was in my pocket and I toyed with the idea of stopping at Betts' place to see if she wanted to take in a movie, but at the last minute I found myself walking past her house and going straight home. I felt irritable and frustrated. Mostly, I felt very much alone.

A note on the kitchen table told me that Mom and Dad had gone to play canasta at the Old Folk's Hangout. Actually it's called the Riverbend Social Club, but all the kids at school refer to it by the less flattering name. I got a bottle of applesauce out of the fridge and went to turn on the television, hoping to distract myself from the boredom and general despondency I was feeling. I was just about to pick up the remote control when I heard a knock.

Thinking that Betts was dropping by, I considered

not answering the door. That made me feel guilty right away, and I pushed aside my impatience at the thought of having my quiet time intruded on.

But it wasn't Betts. When I swung the door open, Greg stood there, shifting from foot to foot and looking very uncomfortable. I was so surprised that I forgot I was holding the apple sauce, and when I gestured him to come in it sloshed over the side of the jar and all over the floor.

"Thanks, it looks really good, but I've already eaten," he said deadpan.

I grabbed a roll of paper towel and sopped up the spreading mess, feeling my face get warm with embarrassment. Greg joined me on the floor and helped with the clean-up.

"I can't help noticing that your talents as a hostess are almost as good as your detective skills."

"Something like your ability to tell time," I shot back. "I said seven o'clock. It's past eight now."

"Maybe I had other things to do. Or maybe I wasn't sure I even wanted to come."

"Well, since you did come, you might make some sort of effort to be civil."

"Then I'm sure *you* can give me some lessons in proper social behavior and etiquette."

"I've already told you I was sorry about that. Why do you have to be so nasty?"

"I'm afraid you'll have to forgive me if I don't seem all that delighted to be here. I came against my better judgement, and it was probably a mistake."

It was on the tip of my tongue to tell him that he might just as well go home then, if that was how he felt, but something stopped me. Maybe it was remembering how disappointed I'd been when he didn't show up at The Scream Machine, or the happy flutter I'd gotten when I saw him at the door. Or maybe it was because it felt so good that he was standing there next to me, even if he wasn't being what you'd call charming at the moment. So instead of snapping back at him in anger, I spoke quietly.

"In any case, I appreciate your coming over."

"So what did you want to talk to me about?" His tone hadn't softened, but at least he seemed willing to stay for a bit.

"The fires." Seeing dismay on his face I hastened to add, "I really think I know who's doing it this time."

"I see. And you want to drag me into it?"

"I don't want to drag you into it. I just wanted to run some things by you and get your opinion. You know, see if you think I'm on the right track this time and what you think I should do about it."

"I'm sure there are lots of other people who would be glad to give you their opinions. You might have considered asking someone you haven't insulted in every possible way."

"I did consider other people," I said, doing my best to ignore the cutting remark. "But I don't want to talk to an adult about it, because they might just want to go right to the police, and I think that would make things worse."

"You have other friends. Why not one of them?"

"There's no one I'd trust with this. Besides, you're smarter than anyone else I know."

He sighed. "Well, I'm here now, you might as well go ahead and tell me about it."

I started by explaining how I'd gone through the book his dad had lent me and how I'd made the various lists.

"Go get them," he said.

"The lists? But they have names on them." I felt that I should protect the identities of the kids I'd included as possible victims of abuse. After all, I could be wrong about any number of them.

I hesitated, not sure of what to do.

Chapter Twenty-Seven

"I'm not trying to be nosy, Shelby, if that's what you think." Greg seemed to sense my dilemma. "I just want to see if a particular name is on your list."

"Why?"

"Because the day of the fire at my place I passed someone when I was on my way home. There was something a bit odd about her, though I can't say exactly what it was."

Excitement ran through me and without thinking I took hold of his arm.

"Greg, was it Jane Goodfellow?"

"Yes, it was Jane." He glanced at my hand on his sleeve, and I let go quickly. "Is that who you think is guilty?"

I nodded. "Can you think back, think really hard about what struck you as odd about her that day?"

"I don't know. At the time I was just hurrying to get home, and it wasn't until later that I thought anything about it at all. And then I figured it could have just been my imagination because of everything else that happened."

"Think, Greg!" I implored. "It could be really important."

"I guess," he said slowly, "that it was something about the way she was walking. It wasn't quite natural."

"As if she was hiding something?"

His eyes got wider then and he said, "Yes, that's it. She was kind of leaning to one side. How did you know that?"

"Because Jane got a new coat at Christmas, but then the Monday right after the fire at your place she had another new one." I told him about the conversation I'd had with Betts and how disgusted she'd been by Jane's snobbish attitude in telling Holly that she no longer liked the coat.

"So Holly asked her if she could have the one she got at Christmas, but Jane said she'd thrown it out. Except Jane always gives things she doesn't want any more to Gail. It doesn't make sense that she'd throw out a jacket that was only a few weeks old, unless there was some reason she had to get rid of it."

"Like if it had a burn spot?" Greg caught on immediately.

"Exactly. But that's not the only thing. Do you remember the night you saw me talking to Jane at The Scream Machine? The night after the fire at the Lawfords' garage?"

He nodded and I continued, "Well, Jane has always worn her hair long and parted in the middle, but that day she'd suddenly changed her style to add bangs. I didn't think much of it then except that they were way too short, which made them look dumb. Something about it didn't fit, but I didn't know what until I asked myself, what if she *had* to cut them and didn't have a choice about how long?"

"And that was the day after the fire at that garage in town?"

"The very next day."

He whistled low. "So you think some of her hair got singed and she had to cut it?"

"Exactly."

"I also know for a fact that she was around town the night the Lawfords' garage burned." I took a deep breath and then forced myself to tell him about doing Nick's essay, how he'd been late coming back, and how I'd learned later he'd been talking to Jane.

Greg was silent for a minute, and it was clear that he was thinking, so I didn't interrupt. When he spoke again it was to make a comment.

"I assume you suspect that Jane has been abused

and that this is why she's setting fires."

"It certainly seems to be a strong possibility," I answered. "Of course, it's just speculation on my part, but I think the evidence points in that direction."

"Tell me what makes you think that." He leaned forward, looking directly at me.

"For one thing, she hates her stepfather. I mean, she really despises him. And it's not just a recent teenage rebellion thing either. She's hated him for as long as I've known her. But she never talks about why, like most kids. You know, she doesn't say he did this or that or anything specific. It's just there, this silent hatred.

"And then there's the fact that she never goes anywhere. That makes it look as though someone keeps a really tight rein on her. Like the school formal. She has a dress and she's all set to go, and then she has this mysterious accident and doesn't show up. Most girls would cover a bruise with makeup and go anyway. Was she too vain for that, or did someone make her stay home? And did she really fall and hurt herself, or was it more than that?"

"I don't know much about the subject, Shelby, but I think it's common for abusers to keep their female victims from a lot of social activities, especially if there are boys involved. It's like some kind of twisted jealousy thing."

I shuddered at the thought of that. It was gross!

"And last year's school picnic - Jane was there for a little while, but then her stepfather came and made her leave. Or the fact that Nick broke up with her because *she* never wanted to go anywhere. Was that true, or was she just saying it to cover up the fact that she's not allowed to go places?"

"Anything else?"

"Well, Jane has no best friends. She hangs out with a group of girls at school to some extent, but she's not close to anyone. You never hear of her going to someone's house or inviting anyone to hers." I explained what I'd learned about secrecy and withdrawing from others being symptoms of victims of sexual abuse.

"And she doesn't do as well in school as she could, not by a long shot." I went on and told him about the academic problems and about her sleeping in class sometimes and the possibility that it pointed to depression.

"You've really done your homework on this," Greg said when I'd finally finished explaining everything. "With the jacket and haircut, and her having been near my house a short time after the shed was set on fire, I think the evidence is pretty compelling."

"But it doesn't *prove* anything," I sighed. "And without proof, what can be done?"

"First of all, what do you think should be done? You mentioned earlier that you didn't want to tell an adult because of the possibility that the police would be called. I take it that you don't want to talk to the police about it."

"Oh, I know that if she's guilty, she's probably going to end up being charged. I just think that she needs help more than she needs a criminal record. What would being arrested and charged do to her? It would only add to the pain she already has to live with. There must be a better way."

"I'm a bit surprised at the way you're talking, Shelby. To be honest, I didn't think you particularly liked Jane."

"I didn't," I admitted. "At least not until I started learning some of this stuff. It gave me a whole new perspective, not just towards her but towards some other girls as well. It must be awful to have to live with that kind of burden, keeping it inside all the time and feeling like you're so alone."

"It takes a lot of intelligence to challenge your own views like that."

"I've found my views have changed about a few things lately," I said quietly. "It's been quite a year so far."

"For one thing, the guy you wanted finally asked you out. Why'd you turn him down?"

"The real question is, what did I ever see in him?" I smiled ruefully. "I honestly can't figure out why I ever liked Nick. Yes, he's good looking and all, but he's so wrapped up in himself. He acts as if other people only exist so they can admire him and do things for him."

"Well, good for you. I wouldn't like to see you dating someone who's so obviously wrong for you. Maybe the next guy who catches your interest will be an improvement."

Before I could find an answer for that, he went on, "Anyway, that's nothing to do with what we're supposed to be figuring out, which I guess is basically what to do about this whole Jane situation."

"That's where I get stuck," I said. "What to do. Any suggestions?"

"Actually, yes. I think there's a good chance that this can be handled in a way that will help her."

He explained what he thought should be done, and how. His idea was surprisingly simple.

And yet, I thought, it just might work.

CHAPTER TWENTY-EIGHT

The tricky part of Greg's plan was going to be to get Jane alone somewhere. I'd never been friends with her, and the time she'd asked me to meet her at The Scream Machine was the only time we'd ever spent any time talking alone.

Greg and I quickly ruled out any place public. Privacy was essential, since there was no way of knowing how she might react. After talking it over, we came up with the idea that I should call her and ask her to meet with me at the corner of Greg's street.

I felt kind of guilty making the phone call, seeing as how I'd never called Jane before. I must have cleared my throat a dozen times before I finally dialed.

"Yeah?" a gruff male voice answered, nearly sending me into a panic. I clutched the phone tighter and asked to speak to Jane.

"Who's this?"

"Uh, my name is Shelby. I'm a friend of Jane's from school." That was a stretch, but I didn't know what else to say.

Instead of him telling me to hold on or anything, there was a clatter of the phone being dropped on a hard surface, followed by silence. I waited.

"Hello?"

"Oh, hi. Jane?"

"Yes. Who's this?"

"It's Shelby."

"What do you want?" Although her words seemed a bit rude, her tone was only curious.

"I need to talk to you. Are you busy right now?"

"Not really, but, uh," she paused, lowering her voice to a whisper, "is this about Nick?"

"No. I can't talk about it on the phone, but it's important."

"Oh, the English project, yeah. Well, I guess I could come over for a little while." She was speaking loudly now, but what she'd said didn't make sense.

"Huh?"

"What's your address then, Shelby? I'll come over and we can get that part of the English project done."

"Not at my house," I protested, trying to follow what she was saying.

"So, where are you at?" she asked in a bright, false voice.

"Can you meet me at the corner of Birch and Princess streets in fifteen minutes?"

"Yes, sure. I know where that is." Another pause. "Okay, so what color is your house? Great. Just watch out the window for me in case I miss it. I'll just get my books together and be along in about fifteen minutes then." She hung up before I could say anything else.

I shook my head, unsure whether she was actually meeting me where I'd asked or coming to my house. Since she hadn't waited for an address or anything I guessed she meant to meet me at the corner. I quickly dialed Greg and gave him a rundown of the conversation.

"Sounds like she had to come up with some bogus story about schoolwork in order to get out of the house," he commented. "That's pretty sad. But anyway, she said she'd be there?"

"Yes."

"Okay, good luck. I'll be here."

I ran a good deal of the way over to make sure I got there in time. There was no sign of Jane when I arrived, but she came along a few minutes later, carrying her book bag.

"Sorry about the stuff about school," she said as she reached me. "My mom wanted me to help clean house this afternoon so I had to come up with a reason to get away."

"No big deal," I said as casually as I could. My heart was pounding hard and I tried not to let her see that I was nervous about anything.

"So, what's up? What did you want to talk to me about? You sure it's not Nick?"

"Nothing to do with Nick. Actually, Greg and I need to talk to you about something. He's waiting for us at his place."

"Greg Taylor?"

"Yes. It's just down the street here a little way."

"I'm not going to his place." She stood looking at me strangely. "You didn't say anything about that on the phone."

"Well, it seemed less complicated just to ask you to meet me."

"What's this about anyway?"

"I can't tell you until we get there."

"Well, then I guess you won't be telling me at all, 'cause I'm not going."

"I think you'd better, Jane. We either talk to you or to someone else." I was hoping she'd read something ominous in my words, and she must have, because she changed her mind right away. Still, she tossed her head and tried to look unconcerned when she spoke.

"This seems a bit foolish, but I guess it won't hurt to go for a few minutes."

Greg met us at the door and ushered us into the kitchen. The three of us sat at the table, and the look on Jane's face made me feel like putting my arm around her. She put me in mind of a frightened, cornered animal.

"What's going on?" she asked.

"We know, Jane," Greg said gently. "We know that you set the fires."

She paled and clutched the table as if to steady herself.

"I don't know what you're talking about." Her voice trembled as she denied his accusation, but there was no shock or outrage in her words.

"Jane, listen to me, please." I put my hand on hers. "We have proof. But we don't want to get you in trouble. We want to help you."

"What kind of proof?" Her eyes darted fearfully back and forth between us.

"We're not prepared to tell you that just yet," Greg said softly, "but you must realize that it's something solid. We wouldn't be saying these things otherwise."

For a moment it looked as if she was going to walk out. She rose unsteadily, forcing a small laugh, commenting that the whole thing was ridiculous and she didn't have to listen to such nonsense.

"Jane," Greg implored, "don't leave and force us to go to the police."

That stopped her in her tracks. She froze for a few seconds and then sank weakly back into her chair.

"I don't have any money," she whispered just before she burst into tears.

That remark puzzled me until Greg spoke, assuring her that she mustn't worry, we didn't want anything from her. When I realized that she'd thought we meant to blackmail her, I felt horrible.

"Here's the way it is, Jane," I said once she'd calmed herself enough to listen. "We know that there must be some reason for what you did. You're not a bad person, not at all. And we want to help you, not hurt you."

As I spoke the fear faded from her face, replaced by a faint look of hope. She listened as we outlined our plan.

"There are two things we need your word on, Jane," Greg said. "We want a promise that you won't set any more fires, and we want you to get counselling."

"Do you think I'm crazy?" she asked. The tone of her voice suggested that she thought so herself.

"Not at all," I reached out my hand, putting it over hers. "We think that someone hurt you badly and you need to talk to a professional about it."

"How did you know?" she gasped before catching herself. As soon as she'd said it, I could see she regretted the admission. Her eyes lowered and she refused to look at us.

"Jane, it's not your fault." I could see shame on her face, and my heart ached for her.

More tears came then, but they were different from

the earlier ones. She sobbed as if something had broken open and the tears that had been held inside for years were being let loose.

We let her cry it out, and then Greg told her that his father was a doctor of psychology and would counsel her free of charge for as long as she needed.

"I can't get away from home," she said, fear and panic in her voice.

"Don't worry about that. He'll set it up with the school and meet with you there. No one has to know anything about it."

Before she left, some time later, Jane talked to Greg about setting his shed on fire. She explained that she knew people were saying that Greg's dad was the fire starter, and had done it to help clear him. She'd made the phone call so that she could be sure he'd be away from the house at the time.

"I never wanted to hurt anyone," she wept.

"It's all over now," he told her. "Everything is going to be okay."

As we watched her make her way along the road I wondered about that. Was it possible that things could ever really be all right for this poor girl? Whatever had been done to her must have been horrible. I turned back to Greg, realizing something.

"I guess I should have been calling your dad Dr. Taylor instead of Mr. Taylor all this time."

"He doesn't care about stuff like that."

"You really believe that your father can help her, don't you?"

"Yes, I do. It's amazing how much people can survive and overcome, if they get help."

I sure hoped he was right. I don't think I'll ever get the thought of Jane out of my mind. And I know I'll never judge unpleasant people again without wondering what makes them the way they are.

"Well, we did it," I said. "I'm glad your idea worked."

"Me too." He seemed uncomfortable all of a sudden and didn't look at me. A brief, awkward silence grew between us.

"I guess I should go now." In spite of our success, I felt miserable.

"I guess so."

I slipped on my jacket and shoes and opened the door.

"Bye then." I wished he'd asked me to stay for a bit or given me some sign that he felt differently than he had lately. I stepped outside and started toward the street.

"Shelby, wait."

My heart leapt, and I turned to see him coming behind me. He was smiling.

"I'll walk you home."

CHAPTER TWENTY-NINE

I read this book a few years ago about a kid named Trevor who did good deeds for three people, and they were to do the same for three others, and so on. It was called *Pay it Forward*, and I liked it a lot because of the idea that the entire world could become a better place because of something one person did.

I think it's really true, too; you can make a difference, if not in the whole world, then at least where you live. When we first started having fires in Little River it created fear and suspicion and a lot of gossip that could have ended up hurting innocent people. The thing is, most folks weren't looking at the reason for the fires, they were looking at the effect, and that was a mistake.

When I got interested in the whole thing and decided to try to figure it out, my focus was on finding out who was doing it. I have to confess that I didn't much care about why. If Dr. Taylor hadn't lent me the book on fire starters, I would never have come to understand that everything a person does is for a reason.

Who knows, maybe I would eventually have put together the evidence that pointed to Jane without ever learning anything about what caused her to set fires. I'm glad it didn't work out that way. Catching her wasn't nearly as important as helping her, and that was the big lesson for me in all of this.

A lot of things have happened since the day that Greg and I confronted Jane in his kitchen. I have to say that I'm proud to have been a small part of it. The experience has taught me to look at people and events in new ways. I think I was pretty shallow before, though it's not easy to admit that, and I hope I've become a better person. I was quick to find fault in others and didn't put much effort into looking past that. I managed to overlook the fact that my habit of being judgemental wasn't exactly an attractive trait.

Well, Jane saw Greg's dad twice a week for almost a month before she was finally able to unburden the secret she'd been carrying all these years. I don't know the details, and they're really not important, but I do know that for Jane, the nightmare of sexual abuse is finally over.

Jane's stepfather was arrested, and even though he hasn't gone to trial yet, at least he can't hurt her any more. She and her mom are getting therapy to help them deal with the whole sad mess, and I see a big change in her already. For one thing, she now has some best friends — me and Betts! It's amazing to think that at the start of the school year I could hardly stand her, and now we're hanging out all the time.

It turns out that Jane is a pretty neat person and brave too. After she disclosed the abuse, she started talking to other people about it. She had learned that she had nothing to be ashamed of, that she had been a victim. More importantly, she was determined to become a survivor! Her courage in passing on a message of hope and healing made a difference to other kids too, because some of them have come forward and told their own secrets.

Jane asked me one day what the proof was that Greg and I had talked about the day we confronted her at his house. I was a bit embarrassed to have to tell her that we had been bluffing, and it worried me that she might be mad that we'd lied. Instead, she laughed, gave me a hug, and thanked me!

Then she told me she was going to the police about the fires. While I stared in astonishment, she explained that she knew she had to take responsibility for what she'd done.

"I've learned that living with secrets is the worst thing a person can do," she said. "Whatever they do to me can't be any worse than carrying around the guilt and the fear of being found out someday. I'm going to confess and get it over with."

It turned out that was the best choice she could have made. Even though charges were laid and she has to go to court for sentencing soon, it doesn't look too bleak. Dr. Taylor is going to help by speaking on her behalf at the hearing. The probation officer, who is preparing something called a Predisposition Report for the court, was also kind and understanding. He's recommending that she be given probation, and we're hoping that the judge will agree with that.

Jane Goodfellow set fires, and that was wrong. Her actions caused needless fear and destruction. But out of the ashes came amazing changes, for her and for other people too.

I guess the people of Little River always thought sexual abuse was some horrible thing that happened other places. No one thought it was going on right in our own quiet town. But it was, and now it's easier for victims to speak out and get help.

Still, statistics suggest that there are many others who have not yet found the courage to tell. I know that some of them are scared and ashamed and that it must be really hard to trust anyone enough to talk about something like that. But their silence keeps them trapped and makes it possible for their abusers to keep on hurting them. I hope that the day comes when everyone in the whole world who has ever been abused will find a person to trust and to tell.

It's good to know that after all the suffering, there is healing at the end. Healing for Jane and for Little River.

I guess that one of the best parts of this whole thing for me has been that I learned not to take people at face value. It takes work to get to know someone, to look past things that might tempt you to dislike him or her, but it's worth it.

My relationship with Greg Taylor is a good example of that. I remember how I felt about him before and how I wanted to avoid him because I hadn't taken the time to look past things that made him different from most of the kids I knew. Now I know that those are some of the very things that make him special. He's someone I hope to get to know even better as time goes by.

I knew Greg had finally forgiven me for how I'd treated him when I got an e-mail from him one day after school. At first it looked like gibberish, but after I studied it for a while I saw that it was actually a cryptogram. Once I'd deciphered it, I discovered that it was a funny poem he'd written about a girl named Shelby, who wasn't the worst detective in the world after all. Thank goodness I figured it out, or I might have fallen back into that category!

I'd like to say that Greg and I are dating, but that hasn't happened. I think he's taking things slow, making sure he can trust me. Maybe he'll ask me out some day, and maybe he never will. Whatever happens, I know that he's a friend well worth having, and I hope that he feels the same way about me.

I have to admit, though, that these days when Betts teases me by saying that Greg is the Man of My Dreams, I don't argue with her.

ACKNOWLEDGEMENTS

I once envisioned the work of a writer unfolding in a solitary place where, closed off from the world, marvelous creations could be wrought. Instead, I have learned that the life of a story is dependent not on silence, but rather, on the steady voices of the world.

In the world that is mine, there are many whose voices have influenced my work.

For this, I thank:

My husband and partner, Brent, for his endless love, support and encouragement.

My children, Anthony and Pamela, for inspiring me daily.

My parents, Bob and Pauline Russell, for teaching me to love literature.

My sixth grade teacher, Alf Lower, for planting the seed that grew.

My brothers Danny and Andrew, the Sherrard family, my friends Janet Aube, John Hambrook, Karen Donovan and Mark Rhodes, and my coworkers at Glenelg, for cheering me on.

And of course, my editor, Barry Jowett, for his guidance and unfailing kindness.